INDIANA JONES

THE ULTIMATE GUIDE

LONDON, NEW YORK, MELBOURNE,
MUNICH, AND DELHI

DORLING KINDERSLEY

Senior Editor Laura Gilbert
Senior Designer Jill Clark
Designers Hanna Ländin, Ron Stobbart
Design Assistant Owen Bennett
Editorial Assistant Jo Casey
Brand Manager Lisa Lanzarini
Publishing Manager Simon Beecroft
Category Publisher Alexandra Allan
Production Editor Sean Daly
Picture Researcher Frances Vargo
Production Controller Nick Seston

LUCASFILM

Executive Editor Jonathan Rinzler
Art Director Troy Alders
Keeper of the Indycron Leland Chee
Director of Publishing Carol Roeder

Cutaway artworks by Richard Bonson and Richard Chasemore

08 09 10 11 12 10 9 8 7 6 5 4 3 2 1

First published in the United States in 2008
by DK Publishing
375 Hudson Street
New York, New York 10014

08 09 10 11 12 10 9 8 7 6 5 4 3 2 1
ID079 – 03/08

DK books are available at special discounts when purchased in bulk for sales promotions,
premiums, fundraising, or educational use. For details, contact:
DK Publishing Special Markets
375 Hudson Street, New York, NY 10014
SpecialSales@dk.com

A catalog record for this book is
available from the Library of Congress.

ISBN: 978-0-7566-3500-8

Color reproduction by Media Development and Printing Ltd, UK
Printed and bound by Lake Book Manufacturing, Inc., USA

www.indianajones.com

Discover more at
www.dk.com

INDIANA JONES

THE
ULTIMATE GUIDE

Written by
James Luceno

CONTENTS

Foreword by Shia LaBeouf 6

THE WORLD OF INDIANA JONES 8
Indiana Jones 10
Indy's Gear 12
Life and Times 14

BIRTH OF AN ARCHAEOLOGIST 16
Indy's Family 18
Early Travels 20
High Adventures 22
The Great War 24
Master Spy 26
Archaeology & Adventure 28

THE TEMPLE OF DOOM 30
Temple Trek 32
Lao Che and Sons 34

Wilhelmina "Willie" Scott 36
Short Round 37
Escape from Shanghai 38
Mayapore Village 40
Arrival at Pankot Palace 42
The Banquet 44
Temple of Doom 46
The Thuggee 48
Pankot 50
Bid for Freedom 52

RAIDERS OF THE LOST ARK 54
Quest for the Ark 56
Search for the Golden Idol 58
Temple Trail 60
Marcus Brody 62
Marion Ravenwood 64
Egypt 66
René Belloq 68
The Well of Souls 70
Tanis 72
Race for the Ark 74
Ark Ceremony 76

THE LAST CRUSADE 78
Grail Crusade 80
Fortune and Glory 82
Walter Donovan 84
Elsa Schneider 86
Venice 88
The Grail Diary 90
Castle Brunwald 92
Escape from Berlin 94
Journey to the Canyon 96
The Grail Temple 98
Grail Trail 100

FURTHER ADVENTURES 102
Thunder in the Orient 104
Sargasso Pirates 106
The War Years 108
Post-War World 110
A Professor's Life 112
Mutt Williams 114
Peru Adventures 116
A Cold War 118

BEYOND THE WORLD 120
The Indy Team 122
Designing the Indy Saga 124
Special Effects 126
The Saga Continues 128
Movie Posters 130
Merchandise 132
Publishing 134
Video Games 136
Indiana Jones Time Line 138

Index 140
Acknowledgments 144

FOREWORD by Shia LaBeouf

MY DAD USED TO WATCH a lot of spaghetti westerns. Other than that, I don't really remember my dad watching much of anything else—except for *Indiana Jones*. I was really into it, so it brought my family together. Most of my friends were introduced to the *Indy* films through their parents, too; I think we all felt that Indy is the ultimate man who gets put into the ultimate situations. But he is scared of snakes; he's vulnerable. He's also funny. He's rough around the edges, but he's a really good person and that's the way Harrison is.

Harrison Ford *is* Indiana Jones. When you first see Harrison on the set, you get breathless. The first time I saw him in full regalia was during preproduction: Harrison pulls out the whip, untangles it, greases it, and he holds it—and you're going, "This is so real."

I first met Steven Spielberg when we were doing *Disturbia*. I saw him again when we were doing *Transformers*. After I was cast, Steven just said, "Welcome to *Indiana Jones*." It's wild to be able to talk about Steven and George Lucas. I'm still getting used to it. And when I first met Karen Allen, it was immediate. You get Karen right away, because she's giving you exactly who she is.

Steven and I talked a lot about the script. It takes place in the 1950s, which was a changing time. I always liked the fact that my character's name is Mutt—because he has father figures who keep jumping in and out of his life. You've got a kid who never really had a stable father. He also has a mother, Marion Ravenwood, who has lived a really intense life: always on her feet, always on the move, always in the middle of the excitement.

So Mutt never really had a normal upbringing. The people raising him were teachers and really smart people, and they educated him—but he quit school. He became obsessed with machinery and motorcycles, which became his own solitary time when he got to grow by himself. Nobody really messes with a person who's fixing a bike. The way Steven always explained it to me was that Mutt is a man-boy: a person who on the outside is trying to present himself as something he's really not. He says, "I'm a man—look at this knife, look at this bike."

But then his adventures begin with Indiana Jones. At one point we're in a secret pyramid in Peru being chased by warriors. We've also been crawling around in caves and cemeteries with skeletons, chased by Russians, and fighting with swords. But you never want that stuff to be too scary; you want to keep the humor intact, even in the middle of the action scenes. That's why there's something for everyone in *Indiana Jones and the Kingdom of the Crystal Skull*. Steven's mind just works that way. Steven Spielberg, more so than anyone I've ever known, understands how to make a movie for every single person in the audience.

Now the film is being edited, while Industrial Light & Magic is working on the visual effects and the legendary John Williams is composing the music. It's all coming together . . . . It's amazing and an honor to be a part of something as big and timeless as Indy—something that started years before I was born, which has become such a phenomenon that has touched so many people and is loved around the world. The man with the hat is back— and I can't wait to join him on the screen.

THE WORLD OF INDIANA JONES

HIS NAME ISN'T FOUND in the annals of the Archaeological Society, though his adventures have taken him to the far corners of the world. Nor does his name appear on a list of the world's most wealthy, despite the riches he has held in his hands or that have slipped through his fingers. He has taken more punches to the jaw than a prizefighter, and yet he wears no title belt. And while he has swung across more chasms than swashbuckling Errol Flynn, the only glimpse of him on film is in a little seen John Ford western entitled *Six Steps to Hell*, in which he is dragged behind a covered wagon. Born Henry Walton Jones, Jr., most know him as Indiana, save for his closest friends to whom he is known, with affection, as Indy.

INDIANA JONES

AS MULTIFACETED AS MANY of the fabled gems he has unearthed, Indiana Jones has worn many guises through the decades. To some, he is a mild-mannered, easily distracted college professor; to others, a fearless adventurer who is out of place everywhere but at the far corners of the world; and, to a few, a man of questionable ethics who plunders the past for his own enrichment and who is known to have left broken hearts and disaster in his wake. To his father, he has dodged every problem he ever faced; and yet, to Marcus Brody, Indy's chief benefactor, he is a light in the darkness. That Indy can't be pinned down makes him even more of a mythic figure.

ALTER EGO

With his tweed jacket, glasses, and bow-tie, Dr. Henry Jones might be dismissed as an eccentric academic. But encounter Indiana in the jungle, bullwhip in hand, and he will be afforded a wide berth. One of these two guises is a kind of secret identity, but even Indy isn't always sure which is which.

EVERYONE HAS A WEAKNESS

Owing to the incident in his adolescence when he was pitched into a vat of snakes during a chase through a circus train, Indy has had a fear of snakes that rivals his father's fear of rats. Jungles and deserts, then, might seem the last places on earth he would care to visit, but in Indy's line of work, that's where much of the action is.

ACTION HERO

A chaser of fortune and glory, Indiana Jones is also a scientist and a man of honor. Where his rivals are often motivated by greed and the desire for power, Indy is in search of fact. He is as eager to disprove the claims of true believers as he is to prove to himself that the world is not only bigger but far more mysterious than anyone realizes. While he advises his archaeology students to rid themselves of notions of mysterious undertakings, few are more familiar with the occult than Indy—and even fewer are as quick to embark on a quest for a long-lost city or treasured artifact. Faced with those who would use sacred objects for purposes of evil, Indy has at times been forced to resort to extreme measures.

FATHER AND SON

Indy has butted heads with his father since the day he was born. Headstrong, impulsive, and daring where his father is stern, distant, and pragmatic, Indy has spent as much of his life running from Henry as he has trying to prove his worth to him. The relationship has colored Indy's affairs with nearly everyone.

In reality, Indy is more like his father than he chooses to believe, and certainly as single-minded when it comes to objects of historical value. For twenty-six years after it slipped from his grasp when he was a Boy Scout, the Cross of Coronado called to Indy, becoming a fixation he ultimately put to rest on a storm-tossed ship off the coast of Portugal.

A ROMANTIC AT HEART

Indiana is as much a ladies' man as he is a man's man. Cynicism born of his experiences in the world wars never fully manages to dim his romantic nature. He has held many women in his arms and proposed to a few, but none have captured his heart more than Marion Ravenwood, with whom he goes in search of the Ark of the Covenant. Up to the task of taking as much as she dishes out, Marion will have a profound effect on Indy, haunting and healing him in the years to come.

Indy retracts the bullwhip and dazzles his adversaries with the saber's blade.

ROLE MODEL

Indiana's zeal in the face of often overwhelming odds has made him a figure to admire and imitate. His adventures have partnered him with people from all walks of life, including streetwise kids like young Short Round.

"I'm going to continue to do things the way I think they should be done."

—*Indiana Jones*

I HAVE YET TO MEET A *SHALLOW* CANYON...

HIDDEN TALENTS

...ES TU ABRAZO TENAZ Y DULZON COMO AQUEL...

OOH!

Indy lives simply, but both his tweed and leather jackets mask a desire for the good life. A few of the rare antiquities he has acquired have helped finance his life as a man of the world and playboy, which sometimes requires knowing the steps of a tango or which wine goes best with water buffalo.

A SENSE OF IRONY

Always in over his head, even when he refuses to admit it, Indy has learned that no good deed goes unpunished, and that situations can go from bad to worse to worst case. Even after evading cunning traps, sinister arch-rivals, and flights of arrows, safety means having to share space with a deadly snake. Champagne is best enjoyed with an antidote nearby, the biggest of bruisers will be the most eager to fight, and precipices will be impossibly high. But to Indy, it's all part of a day's work.

Indiana's experiences as a spy master in the Great War were mere rehearsals for the roles he would later play. His fluency in more than a dozen languages and his ability to immerse himself in indigenous cultures enable him to pass himself off as whoever the situation demands he be, whether that's a Nazi soldier or a Scottish lord.

OLDER AND WISER

Indy doesn't mellow with age. Twenty-one years after embarking on the search for the Ark of the Covenant, he is drawn into a quest that proves equally challenging and ultimately just as profound. Beginning at a government hangar in Nevada, the adventure takes Indy and a young companion to the coastal desert of Peru, and finally into the heart of the Amazon jungle— where some lives will be lost and others will be transformed.

INDY'S GEAR

A LIFE OF TRAVEL has made Indiana Jones a quick packer. During the world lecture tour of his youth, he and his parents traveled with enormous steamer trunks filled with clothing to suit every possible occasion. Having grown up watching his father scribbling notes into the small book he carried in his jacket pocket, Indy took easily to recording his own experiences. Illustrated like Henry's Grail diary, Indy's journal includes hand-drawn maps, letters, intriguing references to rumored ruins or riches, and entries that capture the inner workings of his mind.

However, during the Great War, Indy learned to whittle things down to the bare essentials. Ever since that time, he has traveled with little more than what he can fit into an aged, camel-leather valise. A vested suit, bow tie, dress shoes, and eyeglasses comprise his wardrobe for archaeological meetings and university lectures. Nearly everything else in the valise are field necessities of one sort or another, which includes books, maps, and charts that no archaeologist or adventurer can be without.

AN ADVENTURER'S ESSENTIALS

Indy's clothing is as durable as he is. For fieldwork—and whatever else may arise—Indy carries a variety of time-tested items, including a long-sleeve cotton poplin shirt with shoulder epaulets, front pleats, and color-matched buttons; a stainless steel and nickel-silver folding knife, with a handle made of stag horn scales; gloves of soft cowhide leather, with straight thumb seams and a color-matched binding; and a separate belt from which to sling his holster and quick-release whip. In his pouch, which would have originally been used to hold a British-made gas mask, Indy keeps his passport and all-important travel papers; leather dressing for the whip, and gun oil for the revolvers; and sometimes a brush to rid his fedora of dust and mud. Whatever else he needs can usually be found in local market places or bazaars.

Both in the Himalayas and the Andes Mountains, Indy finds his leather jacket handy for sliding down snow fields.

THE INDIANA JONES CHRONICLES

At the start of the world lecture tour, Indy's father presented him with a journal similar to the one Henry himself was never without, though adorned with a cover of embossed leather.

"I'm like a bad penny. I always turn up."

—Indiana Jones

Indy's high-crowned, wide-brimmed fedoras are made by Herbert Johnson of London.

The A-2 bomber jacket was inspired by 1930s models worn by pilots.

MY HAT!!!

In a brawl with a burly bandit on the road to Tripoli, Indy doesn't get really angry until his opponent flattens his beloved fedora.

THE HAT MAKES THE MAN

Indy has an almost supernatural bond with his fedora. As frequently as it blows from his head, he will find it, or it will find him. He has favored the fedora since 1912, when a looter crowned him with one. The hat is made of soft wool felt, sable in color, and trimmed with a sheenless brown ribbon.

Indy has replaced the bag's cotton strap with a stronger leather strap.

When expertly cracked, part of the whip at the end of the throw exceeds the speed of sound, creating a small sonic boom.

Trained in the use of surveying equipment, Indy has no trouble using a transit to zero in on the Well of Souls at the Tanis digs.

WHIP SMART

Indy spent years taming the object that had left him with a scar on his chin in his adolescence. By 1916, in Mexico, he was already using a bullwhip skillfully—against a murderer named Demetrios—and by 1922 he owned one. Indy's preferred model is 3.3 yards (10 feet) long, with a 12-plait thong of kangaroo hide and an 8-inch (20 cm) knobbed handle. Natural tan at the onset, Indy's whips have turned dark brown over the years.

On an Arizona outing, Indy's whip proves useful against scorpions and would-be assailants.

Indy's loose-fitting battledress trousers are made of a traditional cavalry twill.

Heeled with rubber and reinforced by steel shanks, Indy's vegetable-tanned leather ankle boots are lined with cotton.

Years spent bushwhacking through dense jungles with a machete have hardened Indy's hands and sharpened his eye.

Indy's leather holster and button-snap whip holder are threaded onto a leather belt.

The original .455 Webley was designed for use by troops of Queen Victoria in the 1870s, and used black-powder rounds.

STRAIGHT-SHOOTER

Indy's wide-ranging experiences have made him something of a weapons expert, and he can accurately fire anything placed in his hands, from a turn-of-the-century revolver to a World War II grenade launcher.

Despite changes in firearm design, his weapon of choice remains a Smith and Wesson Hand Ejector 2, with a shortened barrel and converted to fire Colt .45 rounds. When things turn ugly, however, he might reach for his Browning highpower. In the late 1930s, he sometimes used a Webley, but ultimately found it too heavy for fieldwork.

Indy has also used a Colt New Service M1917.

LIFE AND TIMES

An early sepia photograph of Indy with his father.

INDY'S LIFE WEAVES THROUGH the twentieth century as if weft to the warp of historical events. If Indy wasn't present at each milestone, he was certainly close. There is scarcely an eminent figure in politics, the arts, and sciences he doesn't meet, befriend, or fight alongside, on adventures that take him from Princeton, New Jersey, USA, to Papua New Guinea.

November 5, 1872 Ulysses. S. Grant reelected President of the United States.

December 12, 1872 Henry Jones, Indy's father, born in Scotland.

March 17, 1878 Anna Mary Jones, Indy's mother, born in Virginia, USA.

May 16, 1886 Indy's future partner in adventure, Rèmy Baudouin, born in Belgium.

1887 Indy's future close friend Harold "Ox" Oxley born in Leeds, England.

1893 Henry Jones graduates from Oxford University.

1897 Indy's Egyptian friend and cohort, Sallah Mohammed Faisel El-Kahir, born in Cairo, Egypt.

1898 Henry and Anna marry.

July 1, 1899 Henry Walton Jones born in Princeton, New Jersey, USA.

1900 Henry Jones Sr. begins teaching Medieval Literature at Princeton University.

March 16, 1900 Arthur Evans locates the Palace of Knossos on Crete.

December 12, 1901 First transatlantic wireless communication sent and received.

December 17, 1903 The Wright brothers successfully fly a powered airplane.

1905 Henry Jr. adopts the name of his pet malamute, "Indiana."

May, 1908 The Jones embark on a world lecture tour with tutor, Helen Seymour, who instructed Henry, Sr. at Oxford University.

June, 1908 Young Indy visits Egypt where he is befriended by T. E. "Ned" Lawrence (later known as Lawrence of Arabia) and accompanies Howard Carter on an archaeological dig in the Valley of the Kings in Luxor, Egypt. Both men have a profound effect on him.

August, 1908 In Florence, Italy, Indy is forced to confront opera composer Giacomo Puccini's infatuation with Anna Jones.

September, 1908 Indy is introduced to artists Pablo Picasso, Edgar Degas, and Norman Rockwell in Paris, France.

November, 1908 In Vienna, Austria, Young Indy falls for Princess Sophie, daughter of Archduke Franz Ferdinand, and receives advice about love from Drs. Freud, Jung, and Adler.

March 23, 1909 Marion Ravenwood born.

September, 1909 Young Indy visits British East Africa, where he accompanies former US President Theodore Roosevelt on a hunt for Burton's fringe-eared Oryx.

January, 1910 Indy meets a young Krishnamurti in Benares, India, and is introduced to Theosophist Annie Besant.

March, 1910 On a sight-seeing tour of China with Anna and Helen, Indy is stricken with typhoid fever, and cured by a celebrated Chinese acupuncturist.

April, 1910 In Russia, Indy is befriended by Leo Tolstoy after an argument sends him fleeing from Henry and Anna's care.

May, 1910 At a remote monastery in Greece, Indy and Henry Sr. are forced to work together to extricate themselves from a life-threatening predicament.

August, 1910 The Jones family returns to Princeton, New Jersey.

July 24, 1911 Hiram Bingham III rediscovers the Inca city of Machu Picchu.

December 14, 1911 Roald Amundsen becomes the first man to reach the South Pole.

1912 Last of the Manchu Emperors in China.

April 15, 1912 The *Titanic* sinks—with Indy and Helen on board. The pair survives.

May 16, 1912 Anna Jones dies of complications from scarlet fever.

Summer, 1912 Henry Sr. and Indy relocate to Moab, Utah, USA.

September, 1912

September, 1912 In a run-in with treasure hunters, Indy acquires a scar on his chin and a lifelong fear of snakes.

1913 Marcus Brody becomes assistant curator of the National Museum.

February, 1913 Indy helps foil a bank robbery in Durango, Colorado, USA.

Summer, 1913 One of Indy's first encounters with Marcus Brody and Sallah sees the trio hunt for artifacts in Egypt, and narrowly avoid being stricken by the bubonic plague.

1914 Moab schoolhouse burns down; Edgar Rice Burroughs writes *Tarzan of the Apes*.

June 28, 1914 Austrian Archduke Franz Ferdinand is assassinated.

September, 1914 Indy accompanies his father to Greece in pursuit of clues to the location of the Holy Grail.

October, 1914 The Jones boys return to Princeton, New Jersey, where Indy attends junior high school.

April, 1915 When his girlfriend is killed by Mexican federales, Belgian Rèmy Baudouin enlists in Pancho Villa's revolutionary army.

May 7, 1915 The British ocean liner *Lusitania* is sunk by a German submarine.

February, 1916 Indy attends the junior prom with Nancy Stratemeyer, daughter of the creator of Tom Swift and Nancy Drew.

March, 1916 On spring break, Indy is kidnapped by Pancho Villa; a letter from T. E. Lawrence convinces Indy to enlist in the Great War.

April, 1916 Indy and Rèmy arrive in Ireland during the Easter Rebellion.

April 5, 1916 The Jones's dog, Indiana, dies of old age.

May, 1916 Indy's marriage proposal to suffragette Vicky Prentiss is declined, and he enlists in the Belgian army under the nom de guerre, Henri Défense.

September, 1916 Indy and Rèmy get their first taste of combat at Flanders, and enlist in the French army when they are sent to the Somme.

October, 1916 Indy is captured by the Germans but manages to escape shortly thereafter.

November, 1916 Indy has a fling with alleged spy Mata Hari.

1917 Russian Revolution.

January, 1917 Indy and Rèmy enlist in the Africa Corps and meet Dr. Albert Schweitzer in the Congo.

February, 1917 Indy is assigned to the Lafayette Escadrille.

6 April, 1917 The United States enters the Great War.

June, 1917 Nancy Stratemeyer marries Indy's junior high school rival, Butch.

8 November, 1917 Vladimir Lenin seizes control of Russia.

January, 1918 Now assigned to military intelligence, Indy has an encounter with a modern version of Vlad the Impaler (Dracula).

July, 1918 Posing as a Swedish journalist in Istanbul, Indy proposes to American school teacher, Molly, who is killed by a spy's bullet shortly after she agrees to marry Indy.

November, 1918 Indy and Rèmy go in search of the Eye of the Peacock diamond.

November, 1918

November 4, 1918 Helen Seymour dies of influenza.

November 11, 1918 Armistice Day.

May, 1919 Indy works as a translator at the Paris Peace Conference, reuniting with T. E. Lawrence and meeting Ho Chi Minh; first transatlantic flight completed, from New York, USA, to Plymouth, England.

September, 1919 Indy returns to the United States to attend the University of Chicago, much to his father's disappointment.

December, 1919 Indy goes on a vision quest in New Mexico with a Navajo medicine man.

1920 Women are granted the right to vote throughout the United States.

January, 1920 Indy and close friend Harold Oxley begin studying under Abner Ravenwood, and meet Abner's daughter, Marion Ravenwood.

April, 1920 Indy develops a fondness for jazz, and learns to play the sax.

August, 1920 Indy inadvertently ends up doing stunt work in a John Ford western film.

March, 1921 Indy forms a fast friendship with fellow Chicago student and saxophonist, Jack Shannon.

1922 Indy gets his first bullwhip; Indy, his close friend, Magnus Völler, and Professor Charles Jacob Kingston travel to Panama on an archaeological quest.

May, 1922 Indy is unknowingly drawn into a plot to topple King Constantine of Greece, engineered by Indy's Sorbonne archaeology professor, Dorian Belecamus.

June, 1922 Indy graduates from the University of Chicago.

July, 1922 Indy takes postgraduate courses in linguistics at the Sorbonne.

August, 1922 On an archaeological dig at Ur, Iraq, Indy meets René Belloq, who steals and sells off some of the unearthed artifacts, damaging the reputation of Peruvian archaeologist Andres Uribe.

November, 1922 Howard Carter discovers the tomb of the boy pharaoh, Tutankhamun.

1924 Indy searches for a unicorn horn.

1925 Adolf Hitler reorganizes the Nazi Party.

February, 1925 Indy is hired to teach at London University, England.

Spring, 1925 Indy and teenage Marion Ravenwood become romantically involved.

Autumn, 1925 Indy and Marion part ways.

1926 El Mirador, a Mayan site, is discovered in Guatemala; first transatlantic conversation via radiotelephone.

February 8, 1926 Birth of Wan Li—Short Round—in Shanghai.

January, 1927 Indy and his saxophonist friend Jack Shannon are cajoled into searching for Noah's Ark by Russian professor Vladimir Zobolotsky and his daughter.

April, 1927 Civil war begins in China between communists and nationalists.

June, 1928 Indy's search for a unicorn horn —an alicorn—takes him from the American Southwest to Fascist Italy.

Spring 1929 Indy assists Marcus Brody in the search for Brody's missing brother-in-law.

October 24, 1929 "Black Thursday," as the US Stock Exchange collapses, starting an economic crisis.

November, 1929 Part of the Jastro expedition to Iceland, Indy meets Sophia Hapgood, with whom he will share several adventures.

1930 Invention of the jet engine; still teaching at the University of London, Indy is asked to investigate the origin of disk-like aircraft that have been harassing and destroying military and commercial planes; aboard a Calcutta-bound train, Indy discovers that Thuggee cultists are using the ancient "City of Lightning" as headquarters from which to overthrow English colonials and to sabotage Gandhi's plans for peaceful revolution.

June, 1931 After Indy returns the Jewel of Heaven sapphire to its rightful owner, he is expelled from Madagascar and warned that he will forfeit a body part should he ever again show his face there.

18 January, 1932 Short Round's parents are killed in a Japanese bombing run over Shanghai, China.

1933 Indy goes on sabbatical from Princeton to help US federal agents recover the stolen Voynich Manuscript, prompting a doomed affair with modern-day druid, Alecia Dunstin.

30 January, 1933 Adolf Hitler is appointed Chancellor of Germany, and launches a global search for arcane artifacts.

March, 1933 Authorities in British Honduras accuse Indy of being a grave robber after he discovers a crystal skull in a Mayan site known as Cozan.

October, 1933 Indy has another encounter with René Belloq at the Frenchman's family castle in Marseilles, France.

November, 1933 Indy teams up with a female missionary and a noted paleontologist to search for a living triceratops in Outer Mongolia. Along the way, he has his first encounters with both Wu Han and gangster, Lao Che, who will figure in his future hunt for a missing Sankara Stone.

March, 1934 In New Orleans, Louisiana, USA, Indy engages in a pistol duel with René Belloq and is wounded in the arm.

April, 1934 Indy discovers an entrance to Ultima Thule—proving the Earth is hollow—under the North Pole.

June, 1934 René Belloq beats Indy to an archaeological dig in Saudi Arabia's Rub al-Khali Desert.

February, 1935 Indy is rescued at sea by aviator Amelia Earhart.

May, 1935 Indy reunites with Wu Han to search for a fabled black pearl known as the "Heart of the Dragon." Later, Indy and Wu Han strike a deal with Lao Che to locate the ashes of Emperor Nurhachi in exchange for the Eye of the Peacock diamond.

May 19, 1935 Indy's close friend T. E. Lawrence dies in a motorcycle accident in England.

June, 1935 When a series of major and minor catastrophes land Indy, singer Willie Scott, and pickpocket Short Round in India, the trio embark on a search for a missing Sankara Stone, which leads them to Pankot Palace's Temple of Doom.

July, 1935 Returning from India, Indy stumbles upon a shrine to the god Mara, known as the Temple of the Forbidden Eye; Indy resigns from Princeton and starts teaching at Marshall College, Connecticut, USA.

February, 1936 In Peru, Indy acquires a golden Chachapoyan fertility idol, only to have it stolen by René Belloq.

March 30, 1936 Last known journal entry by Abner Ravenwood, presumably buried by an avalanche in the Himalayas.

April, 1936 Indy, Marion Ravenwood, and Sallah follow clues to the whereabouts of the Ark of the Covenant.

July 17, 1936 Spanish Civil War begins.

September, 1936 Indy receives Sallah's help in recovering the Chachapoyan fertility idol.

October, 1936 Indy and Marion go to Greece, then to the Shangri-La-like city of Ra-Lundi, in Asia, to follow up on rumors that Abner Ravenwood is still alive.

1937 The Japanese invade China, taking Shanghai and Peking; introduction of the first useful helicopter.

June, 1938

May 6, 1937 The zeppelin *Hindenburg* bursts into flames and crashes.

January, 1938 Indy begins teaching at Barnett College, New York.

February, 1938 Indy and Francisca Uribe journey to Peru in search of the Chimu Taya Arms.

March, 1938 On a ship off the coast of Portugal, Indy finally retrieves the Cross of Coronado.

June, 1938 Indy continues his father's search for the Holy Grail.

July, 1938 Birth of Henry "Mutt" Williams.

October, 1938 Indy foils a Japanese plot to use the Covenant of Buddha for evil ends.

1939 Indy meets George "Mac" McHale, with whom he will later share many wartime experiences; Marcus Brody becomes Dean of Students at Marshall College; Indy goes in search of his former mentor, Professor Charles Kingston.

May, 1939 Indy and Sophia Hapgood hunt for Atlantean artifacts.

September 3, 1939 Britain and France declare war on Germany.

December, 1939 Indy joins the Office of Strategic Services.

1941 Indy searches for the Golden Fleece.

June, 1941 Indy investigates claims that a golden valley has been discovered in the Bolivian Amazon.

December 7, 1941 Japan attacks Pearl Harbor, Hawaii.

May, 1942 Still working with the OSS, Indy teams up in Flensburg with MI6 operative George McHale.

September 3, 1943 Italy surrenders after Allied invasion.

June 6, 1944 D-Day: Allied forces land at Normandy.

1945 Indy and Henry Sr. search for the Spear of Destiny.

August 6, 1945 First use of an atomic bomb.

September 2, 1945 World War II ends.

1946 Beginning of the "baby boom" generation.

1947 Dead Sea Scrolls discovered near Jerusalem; Indy and Sophia Hapgood search for the Infernal Machine.

July 9, 1947 The US Air Force brings Indy to Roswell, New Mexico, to investigate the crash of an exotic aircraft.

August 15, 1947 India becomes independent and splits, forming India for Hindus and Pakistan for Muslims.

30 January, 1948 Mahatma Gandhi is assassinated by Hindu extremist.

1951 Death of Henry Jones Sr.

1952 Hydrogen bomb is tested; death of Marcus Brody.

Summer, 1957

1957 Indy's former classmate and close friend Harold Oxley goes missing in Peru.

Summer, 1957 Indy travels to Peru in search of Oxley and Mutt Williams' mother.

Sophia Hapgood and Indy manage to escape with their lives on their search for Atlantis.

BIRTH OF AN ARCHAEOLOGIST

ARCHAEOLOGY DEMANDS A FASCINATION for the past, a tolerance for tight spots, and the patience for painstaking research. Growing up among academics in Princeton, New Jersey, Indy is exposed to the rigors of scholarship, and his willful nature lands him in a few tight spots. But the die isn't fully cast until the Jones family's world tour. All at once, young Indy is on a real adventure, not a pretend one, experiencing new places and cultures. Here, investigating the past means gazing into a real Egyptian sarcophagus. Indy also encounters sickness, thievery, and murder, and learns that he must accept them as part of human nature and history.

INDY'S FAMILY

BORN IN PRINCETON, NEW JERSEY, in 1899, Indy is the only child of Oxford-educated Henry Jones Sr., Chair of Medieval Literature at Princeton University, and Anna, who hails from a genteel Southern family. Blessed with his father's dark eyes and his mother's ear for music, the boy has also been saddled with the sobriquet "Junior"—he rebels by taking the name of the family dog, Indiana. While Anna dotes on her spirited son, Henry is a strict disciplinarian. He refuses to call Henry Jr. "Indiana," and makes him chew on cloves of garlic when he fails to memorize the ancient Greek myths.

> ### *"You left just when you were becoming interesting."*
> —Henry Jones Sr.

THE TOUGH PROFESSOR

An erudite scholar and celebrated author, Henry Sr. wishes that his son would focus his abundant energy on improving his intellect, rather than collecting baseball cards and gallivanting with his friends. Indy wants to live up to his father's growing legend, but only on his own terms. More and more, Anna becomes a buffer between a father who is more interested in ruins than people, and a son who breaks the rules at every opportunity. With each passing year, the gulf between Henry and Indy widens, until they finally stop speaking to each other.

A photograph of the Joneses, taken in Princeton in 1907. Henry and Anna are as much a product of the Victorian age as Indy will be of modern times.

After Anna's sudden death in 1912, Henry and Indy retire from the world and rent a small, frontier-style home in Utah. For Indy, it beats boarding school.

NOSE IN A BOOK

"May he who illuminated this, illuminate me," Henry whispers, as he continues his studies of the Holy Grail. Despite Indy's belief to the contrary, Henry claims that Anna *did* understand his obsession with the Grail. A religious man and a seeker of truth, Henry never quite gets over his wife's death from scarlet fever, and speaks to Indy only because Anna would have wanted him to.

OLD WORLD CHARM

In 1908, while in Florence, Italy, Anna is romanced by composer Giacomo Puccini. Anna resists at first, but then starts to warm to him. Indy and Helen wonder if Anna will walk out on Henry, who is a professor first and husband second, but the affair progresses no further than a kiss.

HOMESCHOOLED

Helen Seymour, who had taught Henry at Oxford, becomes Indy's tutor for the two years that the Jones family spends touring the world. The daughter of a minister and a fiercely independent woman, Helen thinks of Indy as little more than a nuisance at first. Later, however, she urges Indy to reconcile with his father before it is too late. After a life during which she was sketched by Pablo Picasso, bequeathed a fortune by a rich relative, and survived the *Titanic*, Helen dies of influenza during World War I.

MAN'S BEST FRIEND

Indy has a strong bond with the family pet, an Alaskan Malamute called Indiana. He becomes upset when he learns the dog must stay behind for the two years of the world tour. "Dogs are better than people," writer Leo Tolstoy will tell young Indy when they meet. Indiana dies the year that Indy goes to fight in World War I.

Exposed to the wonders of the world, Indy sometimes feels as if his senses have been filled to overflowing.

Indy's newsboy cap attracts much attention on his world tour.

EASTERN MEDICINE

In 1910, Henry decides to remain in Peking to give yet another lecture. Anna, Helen, and Indy—intent on seeing the sights—decide to travel on their own. While undertaking a long and arduous trip to the birthplace of Confucius, Indy falls ill and cannot be moved. The nearest Western doctor is days away by wagon, so Anna and Helen reluctantly entrust Indy's care to a local acupuncturist. Anna holds her son's hand throughout the unusual procedure. In any event, Indy is suffering from typhoid fever, and the acupuncturist saves his life.

EARLY TRAVELS

THE WORLD LECTURE TOUR THAT BEGINS IN 1908 furthers Henry Jones Sr.'s reputation as a brilliant scholar, fosters for Anna a desire to do charitable work, and fulfills Helen Seymour's wishes to see the Taj Mahal and the Kyoto gardens. For Indy, the tour is a nonstop adventure that acquaints him not only with exotic places, but with extraordinary women and remarkable men. Indy meets as many interesting people on his own as he does with his parents, and each contributes in some way to his thirst for knowledge. By the time the family returns to Princeton, Indy knows that he can feel at home anywhere in the world.

NAVIGATING THE NILE

Young Indy's experiences in Egypt prove formative. There, he encounters Howard Carter, who is already a celebrated archaeologist although he has yet to discover Tutankhamun's tomb. Carter ushers Indy into a world of ancient mystery and magic. In Luxor's Valley of the Kings, Indy begins his first journal, crawls into his first crypt, and views his first mummy. He also becomes involved in attempts to unmask a murderer who will remain on the run from the law for the next eight years—until he and Indy cross paths again in Mexico.

"Archaeologists don't steal from the past; they open it up for everyone."
—T. E. Lawrence
aka Lawrence of Arabia

Indy's suit and pith helmet were purchased at the bazaar in Cairo.

KRISHNAMURTI

In Benares, on India's River Ganges, Indy mistakes a cricket match for a baseball game. In so doing, he meets young Jiddu Krishnamurti, who is being proclaimed a messiah by the Theosophical Society. Though Indy dabbles in meditation, the practice doesn't suit him. He leaves his new friend with a baseball card of the Detroit Tigers' Ty Cobb.

Indy realizes at once that he is made for a life of travel and adventure. Even his camel grasps as much.

LAWRENCE OF ARABIA

When Indy and Helen visit the Pyramids of Giza, their guides abandon them. Preparing for a long night in the desert, they are found by T.E. "Ned" Lawrence, who, like Henry Sr., had been a student of Helen's at Oxford. "Ned," who will become a lifelong mentor and friend, frightens Indy with campfire tales about mummies, but also teaches him a valuable lesson—that learning the native language is the only way to fully experience a foreign culture.

In the tomb Carter has opened, Ned and Indy discover that a jackal headpiece has been stolen.

HEAD OVER HEELS

Taking horse-riding lessons in Vienna while his parents attend the first psychoanalytical conference, Indy develops a mad crush on the daughter of soon-to-be-assassinated Archduke Ferdinand. Princess Sophie and Indy go ice-skating, but their parents allow no more than that. After seeking advice from Sigmund Freud, Alfred Adler, and Carl Jung, Indy sees Sophie one last time, taking with him a kiss and a locket.

Indy is roughly escorted from Archduke Ferdinand's palace. All he had wanted to do was to give Sophie a snow globe containing two ice-skaters—and ask for her hand in marriage.

CONSERVATION IN AFRICA

Indy's experiences in British East Africa (present-day Kenya) provide lessons in ecology, conservation, and tribal life, under the tutelage of former US president Theodore Roosevelt, who teaches Indy how to shoot, and a tribal youth named Meto. Roosevelt is on an expedition to collect museum specimens of a rare species of antelope known as Burton's fringe-eared oryx. With Indy's help, he finally locates a herd of the elusive antelope, but Indy makes him promise to restrict his killing to only a few of the beautiful creatures.

Roosevelt insists that museum specimens educate people about conservation.

With Meto, Indy learns why the oryx has become scarce. Moles now compete for its favorite food, the root melon, after a widespread fire killed off the snakes that usually preyed on the moles.

HIGH ADVENTURES

WHILE INDY'S EARLY TRAVELS shape his childhood, the experiences he has in adolescence set the stage for what is to come in his adult life. One significant adventure occurs in southern Utah, where Indy and Henry Sr. are living following the death of Indy's mother. In part as a consequence of his growing estrangement from his father, twelve-year-old Indy falls in love with the outdoors. He hikes, rides, and earns the rank of Life Scout in the Boy Scouts. On one occasion, scoutmaster Havelock leads Indy's troop to a place in the middle of the high desert known for its amazing wind-sculpted rock formations, once the haunt of American Indian medicine men, Spanish conquistadors, and prospectors.

GRAVE ROBBERS

Exploring a gaping cave, Indy and his friend Herman chance upon four men excavating an ancient artifact from a burial site. Indy recognizes the Cross of Coronado from one of Henry's textbooks and decides that it belongs in a museum. He sends Herman to alert the scoutmaster and local sheriff, then sneaks down into the cavern and confiscates the cross.

DERRING-DO

With the bejeweled Cross of Coronado tucked into his Hopi-style belt, Indy hurries out of the cave and whistles for his horse. Realizing that the looters are hot on his trail, he attempts to leap onto the horse's back—a trick he has seen cowboys perform—but the horse steps out from under him. Undeterred, Indy dusts himself off, mounts the horse, and gallops away, pursued by the four looters in a truck. Inside a convertible sedan that drives alongside the vehicle, Indy spies a man in a white suit and a Panama hat, who appears to be the leader of the bunch.

> Ignoring the pain in his whiplashed chin Indy inches toward the lion, determined to reach the cross.

Everyone had been waiting weeks for the circus to come to town. Spurring on his horse, Indy catches up with the circus train and climbs aboard.

Cracking a lion tamer's whip is quite a challenge for a novice.

A DAY TO REMEMBER

Chased by the looters, Indy crawls along a catwalk through the circus train's reptile car, past bin after bin of snapping alligators and wriggling snakes. When the catwalk supports give way, Indy flies headfirst into a tank housing an angry anaconda. Rearing back, he falls into one of the bins and all but drowns among its countless snakes. This experience—the basis of his lifelong fear of snakes—will be relived by Indy in years to come.

The crucifix once belonged to the 16th-century explorer Francisco Vásquez de Coronado.

HE'LL BE BACK

Dragged onto the roof of the moving train, Indy faces off with the looters whom he has named Half-Breed, Rough Rider, Fedora, and Roscoe. Fedora grants that Indy has pluck, but demands that he hand over the crucifix. Unwilling to surrender, Indy escapes and exits the train through a trick box in Dr. Fantasy's Magic Caboose. Back home, he tries to interest his father in what has happened, without success.

When the sheriff and the looters show up at the house, Indy is told that the man in the Panama is the cross's rightful owner.

INDY THE IDEALIST

GO!!
GO!!

In New Mexico during spring break, Indy and his cousin Frank pay a visit to a border town. When Mexican bandits strike, Indy goes after them. He is captured by members of General Pancho Villa's peasant army and saved from execution by Villa himself. Fired by idealism, Indy joins the revolutionary cause. During a raid, he throws a railroad switch to direct a dynamite-laden train car into the wall surrounding Ciudad Guerrero.

THE CROSS OF CORONADO

The golden crucifix was said to have been given to Fernando Vásquez de Coronado in 1520 by the conquistador Hernán Cortés. He lost it while searching for the legendary cities of gold. Coronado never found what he was looking for, and returned to Mexico a broken man.

Indy still has the hat that the looter Fedora gave him later.

A MOTLEY CREW

Initially, Indy believes that Pancho Villa is fighting the good fight. So, too, does Rèmy Baudouin, a Belgian who befriends Indy from the start. Indy's disillusionment begins when he hears a campesino say that Villa is no better than any of the politicians who lead the poor into the struggle, then end up stealing their chickens. Later, during a raid on newspaper magnate William Randolph Hearst's hacienda, Rèmy and Indy view newsreels of World War I raging across for Europe. That, along with a letter from T.E. Lawrence, settles the matter. Indy decides to join Ned and Rèmy in fighting the bigger fight.

THE GREAT WAR

Indy's frightening experiences of trench warfare on the Western Front include crawling crater to crater through body-strewn no-man's-land. He survives exploding shells, gas attacks, and German flamethrowers.

IT IS WORLD WAR I and Indy and Rèmy Baudouin arrive in England following their adventure in Mexico. The pair is welcomed into the Belgian army, despite the fact that Indy is underage and has borrowed the nom de guerre (war name) Henri Défense from a poster on the wall of the enlistment office. Awaiting orders and rethinking his options, Indy meets and falls in love with a young suffragette, Vicky Prentiss. Vicky rejects Indy's impulsive proposal of marriage so that she can pursue her dream of being a writer. Rèmy, on the other hand, gets hitched to his girlfriend, Suzette, the day before he and Indy ship out for training at Le Havre, France. Almost immediately the pair are thrown into the thick of the fighting at Flanders, where all the officers in their company die. From these terrifying events, Indy and Rèmy move on to the horrors of the Somme—an experience that will change them forever.

"I hate not knowing what comes next."

—Rèmy Baudouin

THE WAR TO END ALL WARS

Captured by Germans at the Somme, Indy takes the name Lieutenant Blanc, in the hope that officer status will grant him preferential treatment. Instead, an escape attempt gets Indy transferred to a high-security prison at Ingolstadt, Germany, where he is befriended by future general and President of France, Charles de Gaulle. Indy and de Gaulle escape Ingolstadt hidden in caskets (narrowly avoiding cremation), but only Indy makes it to freedom.

De Gaulle tells Indy that the Great War is a turning point. Future conflicts will rely on the concentrated use of armor and aviation.

GIVER AND TAKER OF LIFE

Indy and Rèmy find themselves in the midst of an impossible mission that sees them trekking across the breadth of the African Congo in search of reinforcements. The pair is rescued by German doctor Albert Schweitzer and his wife. Rèmy loses two toes to chiggers (a kind of mite) and Indy nearly dies of fever, but the Schweitzers' selfless missionary work proves an inspiration to the young adventurer.

COMRADES IN ARMS

Indy and Rèmy's horrifying experiences in Europe and Africa forge a friendship that endures through most of the war. Their bond is put to the test when they discover a map on the body of a dead soldier, and embark on an adventure that takes them from Africa to Asia in search of the Eye of the Peacock diamond. Shipwrecked in the southwest Pacific in the Trobriand Islands, Indy and Rèmy are taken captive by a warrior tribe. Eventually they are released into the custody of Bronislaw Malinowski, a Polish-Austrian anthropologist. In his time with Malinowski, Indy faces up to his ambition to return to America to study archaeology, leaving Rèmy to chase his own dream of discovering untold wealth.

Indy is saddened by the senseless killing of a young tribal boy who befriended him. Anthropologist Malinowski explains that the Trobriand tribespeople kill or make war on one another only to appease ghosts, who would otherwise bring blight and disease to the islands.

FLYBOYS

When Indy returns from his adventures in Africa, he lands an assignment as reconnaissance photographer for the Lafayette Escadrille, a French flying unit. Partnered with pilot Harold Green, Indy survives a plane crash and yet another capture. He is also forced to walk out onto the wing of a looping biplane and is involved in a dogfight with flying ace the "Red Baron." Finally, Indy destroys a Fokker-designed triplane that had the capacity to rain bombs on New York City.

Despite feeling drained from fighting, Indy summons enough energy to lead the charge.

SITUATIONAL ETHICS

Passing on a chance to return to America, Indiana serves a stint as a courier for French forces at Verdun, and begins to understand the role that politics plays in warfare. He is disheartened by the attitudes of the French generals overseeing the capture of Fort Douaumont, who are under pressure to end the war quickly—whatever the human cost. On a spying mission, Indy learns that the Germans are moving in two Big Berthas (howitzers) to defend the fort. A suicidal French command to attack is quickly retracted. When another general tries to reinstate the assault with a handwritten countermand, Indy, sensibly, destroys it.

MASTER SPY

BACK IN EUROPE AFTER their devastating experiences in Africa, Indy and Rèmy are determined not to return to the trenches, although they are still deeply committed to the war effort. They transfer to the Belgian army's intelligence division, but before long Indy realizes that they can be far more effective in the superior French intelligence service, and so he counterfeits their transfer orders. Even though the papers are exposed as forgeries, Indy and Rèmy are still accepted, which actually makes Indy question the wisdom of his actions—but not for long. Rèmy's skills as a cook get him assigned as an intelligence liaison at a Brussels café, but Indy winds up in the field, where he encounters some of the most colorful and peculiar characters that he will ever meet and learns the art of disguise.

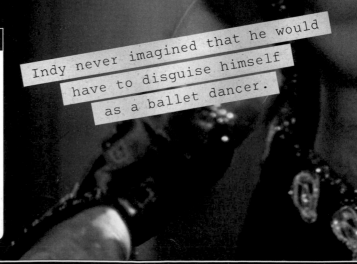

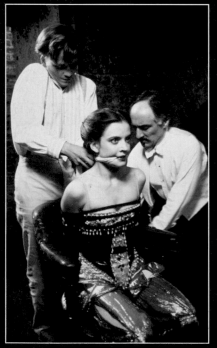

Nadia is bound and gagged after trying to warn Schmidt, but it later emerges that she is an American double agent.

> ### "I assure you, Captain Défense, there is little honor among spies."
> #### —Colonel Waters

ESPIONAGE ESCAPADES

Dispatched to Barcelona, Spain, Indy joins a trio of other agents trying to spur neutral Spain into entering the war. With the help of artist Pablo Picasso, whom he had met during his family's world tour, Indy secures an undercover job with the Ballets Russes, which is staging a production of *Scheherazade*. The plot hatched by Indy and his fellow agents involves fabricating a romance between the Contessa of Toledo and German cultural attaché Schmidt, who is clearly infatuated with the ballet company's lead ballerina, Nadia.

GUILTY UNTIL PROVEN INNOCENT

Indy's first brush with intrigue predates his service as an intelligence operative. In Paris, on leave from the Western Front, he becomes involved with the infamous exotic dancer, Mata Hari. Unknown to Indy, Mata Hari's dalliances with various influential officers have led the French intelligence service to suspect her of espionage. While Indy is in Africa, he learns of her execution by firing squad.

Indy never imagined that he would have to disguise himself as a ballet dancer.

DAREDEVILS OF THE DESERT

On the recommendation of T. E. Lawrence, Indy is sent to Palestine, where British forces, including the Australian Light Horse Brigade, are preparing to take Jerusalem. In an effort to convince the Turks that the British mean to invade Gaza first, Indy disguises himself as a Middle Eastern merchant and is teamed with a beautiful belly dancer named Maya. The pair head for the desert town of Beersheba, where they hurry to defuse explosives in all of the town's wells before the Australian cavalry arrives. While Indy was never convinced that Mata Hari was a German spy, he nurses no such doubts about Maya, who sabotages his plans and nearly kills him.

Indy, Marcello from Italy, and Saul from France put their heads together to hatch a new plan. Working for the intelligence service reveals to Indy the importance of having friends in all places.

A SEPARATE PEACE

In one of his first missions for French intelligence, Indy escorts Princes Xavier and Sixtus of Bourbon-Parma to Vienna, Austria. He wants them to persuade their brother, Emperor Karl I, to sign a treaty with France and Britain. With doubts about its terms, Karl wavers before signing. His foreign minister, Count Czernin, drafts a clever document that will allow the Austrians to deny everything if the German Kaiser ever learns of the secret treaty.

RUSSIAN REVOLUTION

Attached to the French embassy in Petrograd, Russia, Indy falls in with a group of young students. His mission is to learn when the Bolsheviks plan to revolt against the provisional government. Lenin, the Bolshevik leader, is expected to remove Russia from the war, which will free up German troops for the Western Front. Even Rosa, a student who is in love with Indy, refuses to provide the information he is after. When Indy goes with his friends to hear Lenin speak, he is moved by the revolutionary's denunciation of the war.

Indy ultimately learns that his student friends have been misleading him. Regardless, he bravely attempts to save them from the wrath of the Cossack soldiers, who are now working with the provisional government. Four hundred students and steelworkers fall to the soldiers' rounds, and the revolution is put on hold until October.

AGENT OF THE PARANORMAL

In a mission that leaves him questioning the boundaries of reality and the supernatural, Indy is tasked with unmasking the true identity of a Romanian separatist general named Targo. The adventure begins in Venice with a tarot card reading that is fraught with bad omens. After finally arriving at the general's mountaintop castle in Transylvania, Indy encounters ball lightning, bleeding ceilings, reanimated bodies, and vivisection. He also nearly has his blood drained by General Targo, whom some suspect of really being Vlad the Impaler—the fifteenth-century folk hero who inspired the fictional character of Count Dracula. When a fall from a great height doesn't kill Targo, Indy and his knife-throwing partner, Maria, lure the vampire to a crossroads, where they succeed in driving a wooden stake through his heart.

ARCHAEOLOGY & ADVENTURE

INSTEAD OF RECEIVING A HERO'S WELCOME on returning to Princeton, New Jersey, Indy learns that his high school girlfriend has married his old rival, his father has grown even more distant, and his native land has become unrecognizable. Indy's decision to enroll at the University of Chicago, not Princeton, only further strains his relationship with Henry. Indy's Chicago experiences shape him as a hybrid academic and rough-and-tumble adventurer. Even Henry will one day remark that Indy's unique brand of archaeology—a far cry from the tried-and-true method of working with picks, shovels, and brushes—is the understandable outcome of Indy's undergraduate years.

Indy comes to realize in the Congo that a map does not indicate the reality of the terrain, or the hardships involved in a journey.

LESSONS FOR LIVING

Working at the Paris Peace Conference, Indy saw how plans to remake the world took second place to punishing the defeated. He hopes that in Chicago he can at least remake his own world. As historian Arnold Toynbee told him, those who forget the lessons of history are doomed to repeat them.

Beyond a shared interest in Sherlock Holmes, Indy has little in common with his roommate, Eliot Ness, future FBI agent. Their relationship worsens when Indy takes up the saxophone.

FLIP SIDE OF THE COIN

While Indy is firming up the moral compass that will guide him for the rest of his life, René Belloq, the Frenchman who will someday be his arch-rival, has already decided that honor is an overrated virtue. Belloq studies archaeology the way a pirate studies a treasure map. Nothing must stand in the way of his financial gain.

With men dying of disease each day, Indy fears that he isn't cut out for leadership.

HOLLYWOOD FOLLIES

In order to cover his tuition costs, Indy is always on the lookout for lucrative job opportunities. The summer of his freshman year he lands a position in Hollywood, working for the producer Irving Thalberg at Universal Studios. When Indy fails to outsmart director Erich von Stroheim at his own game, he ends up standing in for a stuntman in a John Ford western movie. He returns to Chicago with his leg in a cast, but at least his pockets are stuffed with cash.

THE LIGHTS OF BROADWAY

Though Indy has been hired as assistant stage manager for a Broadway musical called *Scandals of 1920*, he devotes most of his time in New York to dashing between the three girls he is seeing: journalist Kate, debutante Gloria, and struggling actress Peggy. When Indy's juggling act is finally exposed and the three girls learn of each other's existence, they serve him his just desserts—they push his face into the cake being served at his 21st birthday party.

ROARING TWENTIES

Indy's job at Colosimo's Restaurant in Chicago takes an unexpected turn when the owner, Big Jim, is gunned down in the doorway. One of the reporters who covers the murder turns out to be Ernest "Ernie" Hemingway, whose devotion to writing matches Indy's passion for archaeology. While Eliot Ness is also interested in solving the case, Ernie does most of the legwork, discovering that the chief suspect is a New York gangster named Al "Scarface" Capone. Embittered by the breakdown of the murder case, Ernie leaves Chicago for Paris, and Indy quits his job.

SCARFACE

Indy is dismayed to learn that Colosimo's murder was prompted by his refusal to become involved with the illegal liquor trade, otherwise known as bootlegging, which is highly profitable now that Prohibition is in full swing. Police Chief Garrity's reluctance to investigate the case further suggests to Indy that Garrity is involved. But the worst is yet to come: When Big Jim's nephew, Johnny Torrio, gives Capone the run of Indy's favorite jazz speakeasy, the Four Deuces, it effectively ends Indy's chance to perfect his sax playing.

> *"Only a fool wastes time searching for something he doesn't need."*
> —*Bronislaw Malinowski*

Indy never would have guessed that his acquaintances in Chicago would run the gamut from hoodlums like Al Capone to writers like Hemingway and Ben Hecht.

HOPELESS DIAMOND

During his quest for the Eye of the Peacock diamond, Indy comes into contact with two single-minded women: an adventuress named Lily and a pirate named Jin Ming, both of whom will die in pursuit of the diamond. After three years of war, Indy understands dying for a cause, but he finds no justification if the cause is greed. When he realizes that avarice has infected his own quest, Indy abandons it and pursues his archaeological dream—which does not depend on a diamond for fulfillment.

THE TEMPLE OF DOOM (1935)

INDIANA JONES HAS BEEN PERSUADED, duped, and conscripted into venturing where greater men fear to tread. Arriving in a remote corner of India after a succession of misfortunes, he is informed that a Hindu god has delivered him there, and that it is his destiny to infiltrate a blood-drenched palace of depravity. Pankot Palace is the epicenter of a malevolent force that is perched to sweep like a storm across the land. It has fallen into the hands of sadistic cultists who think nothing of sacrificing the lives of innocents to achieve their ends. The darkest of Indy's journeys finds him enslaved to a power he thought no longer existed and compelled to participate in a gruesome ritual that tests the very fiber of his being. In the end, Indiana is forced to risk his heart and soul to retrieve a sacred stone and to rescue a youngster he scarcely knows, a nightclub singer he has just met, and a group of missing children he has never seen.

TEMPLE TREK

In HIS 1935 ADVENTURE IN INDIA, Indy endures enough close calls to pepper a dozen such exploits. In a short space of time, he is poisoned, shot at, compelled to leap from an aeroplane, obliged to eat maggoty rice and chilled monkey brains, forced to drink blood, whipped and beaten, assailed by swords and flights of arrows, and left to the mercy of a madman determined to pluck out his heart. Defying death at every turn, Dr. Jones logs less than his usual number of horizontal miles, but even those few accrue in an inflatable raft, on the back of an elephant, and inside an out-of-control mine car.

ELEPHANT RIDE

The Asian elephant is smaller than its African cousin, but its hair is coarse enough to poke through even the thickest of fabrics. Stuffed with dried reeds and coconut fibers, the saddle and undersaddle—*gaddi* and *namda*—afford some measure of protection, but then there is the grueling nature of the ride itself, with the pachyderm's bone shifting beneath its tough skin and his giant eyes drawing gnats, flies, and sweat bees.

MAYAPORE VILLAGE

NEW DELHI

PANKOT PALACE

INDIA

ARABIAN SEA

PINDARI GLACIER, India

Well-known to climbers who have attempted to summit the Indian Nanda Devi peak—more than 20,000 feet (6,096 m) high—the Pindari Glacier spills down from the valleys of the Kumaon Himalayas and gives rise to an eponymous river that surges southwest toward Delhi. The area is dotted with the stacked-stone huts of hermits and holy men, and word has it that the rhododendron forests may harbor an abominable snowman.

KEY

❶ Indy, Willie Scott, and Short Round escape Club Obi Wan by car. They leave Shanghai on Lao Che's Ford Trimotor cargo plane

❷ Short Round had been instructed to procure three tickets to Bangkok and that's where the trio thinks they are headed

❸ Chungking, in central Asia, is one of several refueling stops for the Ford Trimotor

❹ Unknown to the passengers, the pilot and co-pilot bail out over the Siwalik foothills, taking the extra parachutes with them

❺ Indy and company abandon ship in an inflatable raft, sliding down the Pindari glacier into the Pindari River

❻ Indy, Willie, Short Round, and their guides walk to Mayapore, then travel by elephant to Pankot Palace on the Yamuna River

SIWALIK RANGE

South-flowing rivers have cut gorges through the east-west mountain chain known as the Siwalik. The rivers cascade through forested bands of rock and soil eroded from the mountains; then level out on reaching the terai, a zone of clay and sand that extends all the way to India's vast alluvial plains. Fossils of the ape-like Ramapithecus have been found in abundance in the Siwalik.

GREAT WALL, China

In addition to being eroded by wind and picked apart by country folk in need of building materials, China's "infinitely long wall" is lately the subject of a hoax originally concocted at the turn of the century by a couple of bored journalists. They claimed that China was accepting bids from American companies interested in demolishing the wall and replacing it with a road. Now a new twist has been added, to the effect that publication of the original story fueled the Boxer Rebellion (1899-1901).

SHANGHAI

While the Japanese naval bombardment of a few years back failed to put a dent in this city's snazzy nightlife, it did leave a lot of orphaned kids to fend for themselves on the streets. Some have found their way into crime gangs that flourish here and that control gambling, prostitution, and the drug trade. Listen closely while wending through the Bund area and you can hear Yiddish as often as Mandarin or the vernacular Shanghainese—the result of an influx of Jewish refugees fleeing Hitler and his ilk in Europe.

CHUNGKING

1 SHANGHAI, China

EAST CHINA SEA

3

CHINA

SOUTH CHINA SEA

BAY OF BENGAL

FORD TRIMOTOR

With less than 200 craft produced between 1925 and 1933, it's a shame to see even one Ford Trimotor go to waste—crime boss Lao Che must have money to burn. The craft's sheet-metal body and corrugated aluminum wings gave the craft its nickname—the Tin Goose—but pilots Charles Lindbergh and Amelia Earhart have sung its praises. The plane has a range of only 500 miles (804.5 km), but tired travelers, or those recovering from doses of poison, have been known to sleep through the refueling stops.

2

BANGKOK, SIAM

LAO CHE AND SONS

LAO CHE'S ELEGANT ATTIRE—the silk brocade dinner jacket and golden-falcon pinky flasher—belie his roots as just another of Shanghai's petty thieves and loan sharks. But Lao Che was gifted with a keen intellect and a ruthless streak that quickly elevated him to the top among the corrupt city's crime bosses. Now he controls businesses on both sides of the law, including pharmaceutical and import/export companies, as well as posh nightclubs like the Lotus Eaters and Club Obi Wan, where American music is served up by big bands fronted by pretty, blonde singers. Never far from Lao Che's side are his two sons, lethal Chen and baby-faced—but equally dangerous—Kao Kan.

Chen and Kao Kan serve as the chief lieutenants of their father's organization. Mayhem is their stock in trade.

A FAMILY AFFAIR

Early in his career, Lao Che demanded cremation ashes as collateral for the loans he floated, thus keeping the souls of his clients' family members in limbo until the loans were repaid in full. Since then, Lao Che has become a collector of rare and royal ashes, like those of Nurhachi, first emperor of the Manchu Dynasty. Lao Che hires Indiana Jones to locate these particular ashes in return for the Eye of the Peacock diamond. However, Lao Che's hunger for Nurhachi gets the better of him. He sends Kao Kan to subvert the deal he has struck with Indiana Jones, by stealing the ashes Indy has gone to great lengths to find. But Kao Kan fails in his mission, paying for the attempt with his left forefinger.

> ## "Congratulations, Dr. Jones. You have won. Let us drink to your health."
> —*Lao Che*

TURNING THE TABLES

Indy and his partner, Wu Han, have crossed paths with Lao Che before, when Indy was in China pursuing rumors of a living dinosaur, so they know to be on guard. When Kao Kan draws a revolver, Indy is quick to yank Lao Che's girlfriend, Willie Scott, to his side, pressing a long-pronged fork into her ribs and demanding that Lao Che honor the terms of their transaction.

Willie is disappointed to learn that the suave Dr. Jones is just another gorilla in a dinner jacket.

EYE OF THE PEACOCK

The table's lazy Susan rotates Lao Che's half of the bargain to Indy: the Eye of the Peacock diamond, the ancestry of which can be traced to Alexander the Great. Staring into the faceted stone, Indy reflects on his final adventure with Rémy Baudouin, his friend from the Great War years. The pair pursued the legendary diamond from the battlefields of Europe to an ancient temple in Sumatra, to the islands of the South Seas.

FLOOR SHOW

Mocking laughter from Lao Che and his sons is a signal to Indy that the deal hasn't been fully concluded. In fact, Indy has unwittingly downed a glass of poison. Reeling back from the table in a frantic search for the antidote, Indy becomes the scariest thing on the dance floor. He punches a cigarette girl in the jaw and frightens the chorus line dancers into flight. At the same time, Willie scrambles after the Eye of the Peacock, which, along with the vial, is kicked across the floor by the shuffling feet of the patrons fleeing for the exits.

SKEWERED BY SKEWER

When Wu Han reveals a gun, Chen shoots first, timing his shots to coincide with the popping of champagne corks at a nearby table. A weakened Indy musters enough strength to hurl a skewered pigeon-flambé straight into Chen's chest to avenge the death of his old friend.

Lao Che's younger son, Kao Kan, has earned a reputation for acts that border on sheer lunacy.

THE GONG SHOW

Indy survives an onslaught by assassins wielding spears and battle-axes. As he takes refuge behind a giant gong, Kao Kan grabs hold of a tommy gun and begins to spray the club with bullets. With a broadsword borrowed from a wooden statue of a Chinese warlord, Indy severs one of the cables that support the gong, and scoops Willie into his arms as the disk rolls toward an upper-story window.

"No one kills my friend and lives to gloat about it."

WILHELMINA "WILLIE" SCOTT

OR WILLIE SCOTT, the granddaughter of a stage magician, Shanghai was scarcely the Hollywood she craved. But what with her gig at Club Obi Wan and Lao Che for a sugar daddy, Willie could have been doing a lot worse. Indeed, New York and Chicago had been washouts due to the Depression and a series of men who had been more interested in sweet-talking Wilhelmina Scott, former beauty contest winner, than supporting the talents of Willie Scott, singer, dancer, and budding actress. Going to the Orient was a gamble, but one that had paid off—in the form of lavish parties, a place of her own, and a growing reputation. But it takes only minutes for Indy to bring it all crashing down around her ears.

Willie rescues the vial of antidote that Indy needs. She hopes to trade it for the Eye of the Peacock diamond.

THROWN FOR A LOOP

For someone who has grown accustomed to riding in limousines, the back of an elephant is torture of the cruelest sort. But Willie is still a lady, after all, and she has a bottle of expensive perfume to prove it. Dabbing some behind her ears, she pours the rest onto the elephant. While it may be the beast that needs a bath, it's Willie who gets one when the elephant pitches her headlong into a stagnant pool of muddy water.

Even though her parents were chicken farmers, Willie prefers indoor parties to the great outdoors.

"I'm a singer! I could lose my voice!"
—Willie Scott

BED BUGS

It takes Willie a few moments to realize that the crispy things on the floor and walls of Pankot Palace's secret tunnel are huge bugs. Even so, she overcomes her revulsion long enough to pull the lever that saves Indy and his sidekick, Short Round, from being impaled on spikes.

SHOWSTOPPER

Willie has tap-danced her way into the mouths of fire-breathing dragons, but those were made of papier-mâché. Buffalo-horned Kali Ma priest Mola Ram is all too real, and he has costumed Willie as a Rajput maiden for her tour of hell. Spread-eagled in an iron cage that resembles a giant waffle iron, Willie can feel Mola Ram's clenched hand tug at her heart. Unaware that Indy has been forced to drink the blood of the goddess Kali Ma and is now in a black sleep, Willie pleads with him to help her.

SHORT ROUND

ELEVEN-YEAR-OLD SHORT ROUND, born Wan Li, was raised in the back alleys of Shanghai after his parents were killed in a Japanese bombing raid. A modern-day Robin Hood, he justifies his talents for pickpocketing as a means of redistributing wealth. Dressed in quilted pants, a Mandarin-collared jacket, and a New York Yankees baseball cap, young Short Round learned English by watching foreign films at the Tai-Phung Theater. Now he dreams of going to America with Dr. Jones, whose bullwhip ensnared him after he attempted to lift Indy's wallet in front of the Gung-Ho bar in the Place of Doves.

Aces up the sleeves and fights in Mandarin Chinese are common when Indy and Short Round play poker.

THE LONG AND THE SHORT OF IT

Trusty and reliable, Short Round is waiting in front of Club Obi Wan when Indy and Willie Scott literally drop into the back seat. The cream-colored 1934 Duisenberg Auburn convertible belongs to his Uncle Wong, but the wooden blocks affixed to the accelerator, brake, and clutch pedals are Short Round's own doing, with some help from Dr. Jones. At first Short Round isn't sure how he feels about Willie Scott—she makes a lot of noise and she's not very good on her feet, despite being a dancer. But she is pretty in an American way, and could be the perfect wife for Dr. Jones—and the perfect adoptive mom for Short Round.

Short Round has been taking driving lessons from Indy, but has learned most of his tricks from gangster movies.

THERE GOES MY HERO

Short Round doesn't think of himself as Dr. Jones's charge, but as his bodyguard. So when it comes to rousing Indy from the sleep of Kali Ma, Short Round is there with a torch to shock him back to reality. He is more than willing to accept a backhand across the face, because he loves Indy with his whole heart.

Even a plucky eleven-year-old can be caught off guard and scream like a child when faced with becoming lunch for a gang of ravenous crocodiles.

Indy had tried to figure out a way to cut the kid loose, but the baseball cap kept getting to him.

ESCAPE FROM SHANGHAI

WITH CLUB OBI WAN'S WINDOW shattered by the giant gong, Indy and Willy's escape route is clear. The awnings slow their descent and the pair crash-land into the back seat of a car driven by Short Round. Lao Che and his henchmen are in hot pursuit as Short Round speeds through Shanghai's streets, plowing through market places and upending rickshaws. In the back seat, Indy downs the vial of antidote Willie had tucked into her gown, and fires his revolver at his pursuers.

1 THE TRIO HEAD FOR *Nang Tao Airport, where Short Round has already arranged for three seats aboard a flight to Bangkok, Siam. Only later will the fugitives realize that they have actually been booked onto a cargo plane owned by Lao Che Air Freight.*

5 SEARCHING FOR ANY MEANS OF ESCAPE, *Indy finds an emergency life raft. Short Round and Willie grab on to Indy as they prepare to bail out. Willie's scream echoes from the mountainsides as the trio jumps from the plane in the nick of time, the raft inflating and slowing their desperate descent.*

2 INDY'S FIRST TASK *after shutting the plane door on Lao Che is to change out of his tuxedo into his khaki pants, leather jacket, rugged work boots, and wide-brimmed fedora. Catching sight of the whip in his hand and the holster on his belt, Willie wonders aloud if he's supposed to be a lion tamer.*

3 DEAD TIRED FROM THE PURSUIT *through Shanghai, the plane's three passengers sleep during the long flight across China. They continue to doze even while the pilot and copilot dump the plane's fuel and parachute into the rugged, snow-capped mountains of the eastern Siwalik Range.*

4 PLANTING HIMSELF AT THE VACANT CONTROLS, *Indy teases that it can't be too difficult to fly a plane. But the joke falls flat when the depleted engines sputter and die, and the altimeter needle begins to spin wildly.*

What with the chaos at Club Obi Wan, there's no turning back for Willie.

6 THE PERPETUAL SNOW of the Pindari Glacier manages to cushion the landing. However, seconds later the inflatable is rocketing down the ice floe like a runaway bobsled, bounding over moguls, spinning in circles, and gathering speed all the way down.

7 THEIR PLUNGE DOWN THE MOUNTAIN continues, whipping through a wood of evergreen saplings. Indy expresses relief on finally reaching the tree line. The raft leaps from the snow onto a patch of dry ground, but barely slows down at all.

8 WHAT INDY INITIALLY TAKES for a glacial moraine turns out to be the level summit of a towering precipice. Soaring over the edge, the raft goes into freefall, plummeting in a gentle curve.

9 A TRIBUTARY OF THE YAMUNA RIVER welcomes the raft with a surge of ice-cold spray. Indy, Willie, and Short Round hang on to the raft for dear life as the inflatable is funneled into a stretch of treacherous white-water rapids.

10 INDY'S ATTEMPTS TO STEER the raft are no match for the Yamuna's turbulent whirlpools. Soaked to the skin, Willie now has added reason to hate Indiana, who has already caused her to suffer through an assault of chicken feathers and has made a sequined rag of her expensive gown.

11 AS THE RAPIDS GIVE WAY to calm waters, Indy spies a holy man with a shock of white hair standing on the shore. Pressing his hands together in a Namaste gesture, Indy announces that they are in India.

MAYAPORE VILLAGE

SANKARA STONES

Legend has it that Sankara, a priest of Shiva, ascended to the summit of Mount Kailsa on his quest for enlightenment. There, Shiva presented him with five stones with which to combat evil. The Sankara Stones are marked with three white lines that represent the three levels of the universe and are as smooth as rocks taken from the sacred Ganges. When the stones are brought into close proximity with one another, the diamonds inside them glow in concert.

S EVERAL DAYS JOURNEY BY ELEPHANT from New Delhi, the village of Mayapore is typical of the farming villages in India's remote northwest. Dominated by a towering mount of stone, Mayapore is distinguished by a dome-shaped shrine dedicated to the Hindu god Shiva. The shrine is carved into a boulder the size of a house and shelters a sacred stone known as the Shiva Linga, which Indiana Jones comes to suspect is one of the fabled Sankara Stones. Formerly a place of pilgrimage, the village of primitive, clay-block dwellings grew up after the uprising of the Thuggee cult in the mid-1800s. Some say the village was founded for the express purpose of watching for signs of a resurgence in cult activity.

A VAST WASTELAND

From the Yamuna River, the holy man, Marhan, leads Indy, Willie, and Short Round into a ridge of increasingly barren hills, and down a gutted path to the small, desolate looking village of Mayapore. Indy is mystified by the bleakness of the surroundings. The village's landscape is one of parched soil, bare trees, withered crops, and an utter absence of wildlife or domesticated animals. His gut tells him that a catastrophe has transpired here—a drought, blight, or worse—and that he is about to be caught up in whatever evil befell the place.

As he surveys the devastated village, it strikes Indy that the Yamuna River is thought to be the earthly manifestation of Yami, sister of the god Yama, who sits in judgment on the dead.

A GHOST STORY

The villagers scrape together what little food they have—fly-ridden bits of yellow rice and moldy fruit—and offer it to their revered guests in the home of the village chieftain. When Indy asks for their assistance in reaching New Delhi, Marhan informs him in no uncertain terms that Indy will be stopping at Pankot Palace first, even though it is not on the way to New Delhi. It transpires that the plane crash that the traveling trio narrowly missed was not merely Lao Che's doing. From the palace, an evil force has been spreading like a monsoon over the land, and Shiva has delivered Indy from the sky to combat it.

Indy's misgivings increase when Mayapore's wretched residents pour from their homes to convey their distress in sign language and tears, and implore him for salvation. Oddly, there is not a child among them.

ESCAPED FROM PANKOT

Based on the chieftain's description of the Shiva Linga, Indy suspects that the magic rock could be one of the legendary Sankara Stones. His hunch proves correct when an emaciated child, the nails of his bloodied fingers worn to the quick and his bony back scarred by the sting of a lash, staggers into the village. He presses a frayed piece of ancient Sanskrit manuscript into Indy's hand and utters the word "Sankara." Indy's trip to Pankot becomes all the more urgent when Short Round discovers the tortured child has fled from the evil palace.

POOR GUY LOOKS LIKE A SKELETON WITH SKIN! PROBABLY HASN'T EATEN IN DAYS! AND--

-- HE'S HANDING ME SOME- THING.

S...S...SANKARA!

THE MAGIC IN THE STONE

Marhan explains to Indy that Pankot Palace's worshippers have not only stolen the village's sacred Shiva Linga but kidnapped all the children. They will only be released when the people of Mayapore agree to abandon their veneration of Shiva for the dark goddess Kali Ma. Their refusal to do so has resulted in the well drying up, the crops being swallowed by the earth, the rivers turning to sand, and the animals turning to dust. But with Indy's arrival, Marhan's prayers to Shiva have been answered.

Rather than allow the Sankara Stone to further his quest for fortune or glory, Indy returns it to Mayapore, along with the village's missing children.

A manifestation of the fertility aspect of Shiva, the Shiva Linga helps to maintain the health of Mayapore's crops and well water.

The rescued stone began to warm in Marhan's hands, pulsing with the life force of Shiva.

ARRIVAL AT PANKOT PALACE

SHIMMERING LIKE A TIARA atop a lush mount overlooking the Ganges, Pankot Palace has been home to maharajahs since the 1500s, and, initially, Indy is glad to arrive. A sprawling citadel of alabaster domes and minarets encrusted with lapis lazuli stone, Pankot remained loyal to the Crown during the Sepoy Mutiny of 1857, when an attempt was made to overthrow British rule. But its fidelity was in part a fearful reaction to what had occurred during the height of the Thuggee movement twenty years earlier, when Pankot's temple to Kali was destroyed by British soldiers, resulting in the deaths of more than 300 Thuggee priests.

The Sankara Stone depicted on the manuscript could be Indy's ticket to fortune and glory.

JOURNEY'S END

After two days of hard travel through the steamy lowlands, Indy, Willie, and Short Round reach the outskirts of Pankot. But when their guide, Sajnu, sees a fearsome statue at the base of the palace's mount, he and the elephant wranglers flee, leaving the trio to complete the journey on foot.

A TRAVELER'S WARNING

Indy doesn't want Short Round or Willie to see what Sajnu has found. The stone statue is of Kali in her most gruesome aspect, adorned with offerings of dead birds, withered leaves, and human skulls.

Pankot's rococo design blends elements of Moghul and Rajput styles.

Stained blood-red by the sun, the sky above Pankot is heavy with portent.

STRANGE HAPPENINGS

Flights of giant vampire bats, fattened on blood and streaming to and from the palace, are a familiar and disquieting sight. The surrounding jungle teems with venomous insects, man-eating tigers, lethal snakes, and packs of aggressive baboons, all seemingly drawn to the palace from afar.

AN AMBIGUOUS WELCOME

Courteous to a fault, Pankot Prime Minister Chatter Lal has not only heard of Dr. Indiana Jones, but has followed his career closely enough to be acquainted with the notorious side of his character. For his part, Indy suspects that beneath the tailored Saville Row suit and veneer of civility, Chatter Lal is more than the humble servant he pretends to be.

EYE OF THE BEHOLDER

British military officer Captain Blumburtt has also arrived at Pankot Palace. Talking to Indy, he dismisses the palace's macabre statuary as mumbo-jumbo. But Indy reveals that many of the idols have been recently carved, and have been used in Thuggee rituals. The British may think they rule India, but Indy knows it is the old gods that hold sway.

CHARMING. WHAT IS IT?

IT'S CALLED A *KRTYA*. IT'S LIKE THE VOODOO DOLLS OF WEST AFRICA. THE KRTYA REPRESENTS YOUR ENEMY -- AND GIVES YOU COMPLETE POWER OVER HIM.

Lal cannot imagine where the lost trio of disheveled travelers would look at home.

LAP OF LUXURY

With its marble floors, meditative courtyards, intricate tapestries, and hyacinth-covered pools, Pankot Palace exhibits all the trappings of opulence. Servants are at one's beck and call, and musicians fill the rose and coriander-scented air with beguiling melodies. But behind this facade, something distinctly sinister is lurking.

A high cliff rises from the river and surrounds the palace.

Pankot Palace is like nothing Short Round has ever seen.

"The maharajah usually listens to my advice."
—Chatter Lal

THE BANQUET

At THE URGING of Prime Minister Chatter Lal, Maharajah Zalim Singh has invited various dignitaries and merchants to dine at Pankot Palace. The purpose of the lavish banquet is to advance Pankot's standing among the neighboring principalities. Chatter Lal had not anticipated the arrival of unexpected guests, however, let alone an eminent American archaeologist and a British military officer on an inspection tour. Unbeknownst to Dr. Indiana Jones and Captain Blumburtt, plans are already well underway to keep the pair from prying too deeply into Pankot's affairs.

A merchant tucks into a boiled black beetle and encourages Willie Scott to join him. She demurs, claiming to have had bugs for lunch.

The meal's dessert of chilled monkey brain—served in the original container—proves too much for Willie, who passes out while the rest of the guests go right on eating.

A REVOLTING REPAST

Decked out in formal Rajput finery, the maharajah's many guests are taken with the talent of the court musicians and the beauty of a quartet of dancing girls. In fact, the scene seems much like any other state occasion—until the food is brought out and the banquet begins. Dishes that no self-respecting Hindu would deign to touch, such as snake surprise and eyeball soup, are gorged on with such gusto that Indy feels something strange must be afoot.

Imported python, poached to perfection by Pankot's chefs

STATELY SPIES

Visitors to Pankot Palace are unaware that they are under constant surveillance. Many of the servants and guards have been instructed to eavesdrop on conversations and report their findings to Chatter Lal, who is thus kept apprised of political developments throughout the sub-continent. Sedatives are sometimes slipped into the unusual banquet fare to permit a thorough search of a guest's suite.

The entrée's surprise is a succulent stuffing of live baby eels.

Speech bubble: "-- AND I AM ASHAMED OF WHAT HAPPENED HERE SO MANY YEARS AGO. WE KEEP THESE OBJECTS TO REMIND US THAT THIS EVIL WILL *NEVER* HAPPEN IN THIS KINGDOM AGAIN!"

"I'M... SORRY IF I OFFENDED YOU!"

THE TOPIC IS DROPPED. THE TENSION REMAINS.

UNSPEAKABLE THINGS

The musicians pause, the dancing girls freeze, and the guests fall silent when Zalim Singh interrupts Indiana's probing questions about Pankot Palace to voice his own views about the Thuggee. Until recently he had believed that stories about the cultists were told by adults only to frighten impressionable children. Now he knows that the Thuggee were real, he is ashamed of their existence. However, the boy maharajah is under the sway both of Chatter Lal, who has been slipping hypnotic potions into Zalim's food, and of a sadistic priest of Kali Ma, who is responsible for poisoning Zalim's father, Premjit.

> *"Indiana Jones, this is one night you will never forget!"*
> —Willie Scott

NOCTURNAL ACTIVITIES

Dr. Jones confutes Willie's notion of archaeologists as little men searching for their "mommies," and she's sure that he's had his eye on her ever since he walked into Club Obi Wan. When Pankot's sultry, jasmine-infused atmosphere brings Indy and Willie's mutual attraction into the open, they begin a teasing courtship ritual, prompted by bites from a crisp apple. But neither of them is willing to surrender control. The flirtation barely makes it past a first kiss when Indy is back to playing hard to get and Willie is branding him a conceited ape.

NO WAY TO TREAT A GUEST

Indy and Willie have a bet that he'll be back in her room in five minutes flat. While Jones is busy trying to think of anything but Willie, an assassin emerges seemingly from a wall mural of standing figures and attempts to garrotte him. Awakened by the sounds of the struggle, Short Round tosses Indy his bullwhip. The assassin inadvertently lynches himself when he yanks the whip from Indy's hands and it becomes entangled in a whirling ceiling fan. The hospitality at Pankot suddenly leaves a lot to be desired.

Willie is rendered speechless by the food on offer at Pankot Palace.

THINGS THAT GO BUMP IN THE NIGHT

No one gets the upper hand over Indiana Jones—even when he is preoccupied with planning seduction strategies. He had checked the bedroom carefully before dinner; so, in the midst of his fight, it occurs to him that the assassin could have entered only by means of a secret passageway. Indy bursts into Willie's room and continues his frantic search for hidden doorways or panels. The secrets of Pankot Palace are beginning to reveal themselves.

DON'T KNOW HOW HE GOT IN, BUT I CAN WORRY ABOUT THAT LATER!

TEMPLE OF DOOM

THE OPULENCE OF PANKOT PALACE stands in stark contrast to the murky malevolence of the temple that occupies the heart of the volcanic mountain. A hasty construction compared to the complex built by Thuggee cultists of the 1800s, which later served as a sanctuary for British refugees during the Sepoy Mutiny, the Temple of Doom sits at the edge of a deep crevasse, and is lorded over by an enormous statue of the dark goddess Kali. The felsic lava that spewed from the mountain eons earlier filled the volcanic vents with riches equal to those at Golconda, in central India, where the Hope Diamond was discovered. Now, however, the Thuggee are interested mainly in unearthing the two missing Sankara Stones.

1 INDY FRANTICALLY searches for secret doors by which assassins might access Willie's bedroom. He finds what he's looking for when he pats down a statue and a hidden passageway is revealed.

2 FEELING THEIR WAY down a rock-walled tunnel harboring caches of mummies and crawling with outsize bugs, Indy and Short Round manage to trap themselves in a chamber with spikes that are getting dangerously close to the pair.

3 DRAWING ON strengths she didn't know she possessed, Willie answers Indy and Short Round's desperate pleas for help. She brings about their eventual rescue after suffering a deluge of insects that simply defy description.

4 IN THE HELLISH GLOW emanating from the magma pits, Indy, Willie, and Short Round reach an overlook and gaze down on the Temple of Doom. There, a gruesome ritual that hasn't been witnessed in centuries is underway.

Tower bedroom overlooks gorge

Perimeter of bedroom suite is adorned with lavish murals

Access to secret passageway with a familiar drawing on the wall

Breeze from secret passageway stirs flowers

Doors and spikes are operated by a pulley-and lever-driven system of weights and counter-weights

Wall trigger that Short Round leans against

Circular door shuts off exit

Floor trigger that causes circular door to close

Spikes sprout from the floor and lowering ceiling

Trapdoor is a limb-crushing slab of granite

Steam mingles with fumes of sulfuric acid

This area floods during the rainy season

Willie and Short Round make their way through the lava tunnel

Indy is uncertain just what they will find

Stalagmites and stalactites have formed in lava tunnel

Volcanic vent accesses mount interior

Skeletons of Thuggee who attempted to evade capture by British soldiers in 1830s

Realm of goliath beetles and bat-eating centipedes

Counter-weights

Fissures resulting from thinning of the Earth's crust

Statues of Ganesha, the Hindu Lord of Beginnings

Flayed skins of captured informers and spies on display

Statue of Kali and Sankara Stone altar

Portal for lowering cage into magma reservoir

Acolytes await head priest Mola Ram's appearance

Indy will gaze down on enslaved children from this point

Active volcanic vent reeks of sulfur

Sacrificial bowls used by children for sifting

Short Round will use this ladder to access the temple

Primitive steam engine powers winch and conveyor belt

A 200-carat diamond was discovered here

Starving children mine for diamonds

Cave-in caused four deaths

Brutal Thuggee guard

A crusher where Indy will fight the master of the slaves

Water-bearers for guards and slave masters

Enormous water cistern

Statues date back to the fifteenth century

Maharajah Zalim Singh awaits the ceremony

Thuggee musicians, gong-players, and drummers

Chanting devotees of Kali

Chamber once used for initiation ceremonies now serves as storeroom for musical instruments

Cooled lava contains Jurassic-era fossils

Railway line to mine shafts

THE THUGGEE

THE SECRET FRATERNITY that eventually became known as the Thuggee began its rise to infamy in sixteenth century India. These bands of thieves preyed on unsuspecting travelers, strangling them with scarves or sashes disguised as belts or decorative accessories. Gradually a cult grew up around the assassins, who spoke in a secret language and gathered to worship at secret temples devoted to the dark goddess Kali. Thought to have been stamped out by British colonial forces in the mid-1800s, the cult survived in small pockets, as Indy learned in 1930, when he found a group of Thuggee in Calcutta.

"You will become a true believer."
—*Mola Ram*

DEATH BECOMES HIM

Mola Ram is the son of a priest who survived British attempts to eradicate the Thuggee. He is said to have killed with his bare hands the water buffalo whose skull he wears, and shrunken the human head that protrudes from between the buffalo horns. A native of Bengal, he formed an alliance with Pankot Prime Minister and secret Thuggee Chatter Lal. This led to Ram choosing Pankot as the site for a restored temple to Kali. Ram has brought unprecedented brutality to the cult, introducing the ritual extraction of human hearts and sacrificial death by immolation in magma.

Ritual chanting to the sonorous beating of drums and gongs helps induce a trance-like state in the many Thuggee devotees.

VIVID IMAGININGS

Mola Ram has cemented his authority among the Kali devotees by being in possession of three of the five Sankara Stones, two of which he brought with him to Pankot and one he took from its shrine in Mayapore. During rituals, the sacred rocks are housed in a skull-shaped, king cobra–crowned altar that sits between the feet of a giant statue of Kali. Informed by a passion to avenge the Thuggee against the British, Mola Ram prophesizes that the cult will one day rule the entire world in Kali's name. Once, that is, the two missing Sankara Stones are unearthed from the ruins of the former temple.

Indy watches in fascination. No one has seen a Thuggee ritual in a hundred years.

ONE MORE FOR THE ROAD

Dr. Jones fancies himself a scientist, and brags that nothing shocks him. But when he is captured and forced to drink the blood of Kali from a chalice capped by a human skull, the rationalist in him disappears. His attempts to spit the blood out are quickly dashed when the young maharajah dips an Indy-like doll into the flames of a torch. A rancid amalgam of animal blood and psychotropic herbs, the brew not only plunges Indiana into a living nightmare—it makes a true believer out of him, just as the diabolical Ram had promised.

LIVING DOLL

The maharajah, Zalim Singh, is Mola Ram's puppet since he too was forced to enter the dark sleep of Kali Ma. He has been trained in the sadistic art of fabricating krtya or voodoo dolls, and using them to debilitate anyone who dares to oppose the demonic Thuggee.

INDIANA JONES JUNIOR

Unknown to the intoxicated Indy, Short Round has been placed among the ranks of the children who were captured from Mayapore, deep in the mines below the Thuggee temple. They spend every waking moment digging for diamonds to support the Thuggee cause and searching for the pair of lost Sankara Stones. Failure to work results in lashings—or worse. Some children have even been forced to drink the blood of Kali Ma. Freeing himself by hammering at the rusted shackles that bind him, Short Round behaves like Indy, toppling a ladder to foil his pursuers, preventing Willie from being roasted alive, and presenting Dr. Jones with his signature gear just when he needs it most.

Short Round realizes that it is possible to rouse someone from the black sleep of Kali Ma after magma splashes one of the guards and he quickly becomes himself again.

SLEEPWALKING

Willie was just kidding when she told Indy he could be her palace slave. And yet here he was, refusing to snap out of whatever spell Mola Ram had put on him, and seemingly happy to assist in her death! To Indiana, though, Willie is no longer the princess who sat across from him at the banquet table, but a treacherous sorceress who has seen and heard dark secrets, and now must be prevented from talking. The sorceress doesn't understand that Kali Ma protects all her devotees, who are like her children. In turn, they pledge their true devotion to her by making offerings of flesh and blood.

Vacillating between bravado and terror, Willie finally spits into Indy's face when he places her free hand back into a manacle.

A RUDE AWAKENING

The flaming torch Short Round thrusts into Indy's side reinforces what he has been counseling since Shanghai: "You listen to me, Dr. Jones, you live longer." Chatter Lal is pleased to see Indy strike the brat, and then watch him lay claim to "Mr. Round" as two guards are about to end Shorty's life. What the prime minister doesn't realize is that Short Round has actually brought Indiana out of his daze. Even Short Round isn't sure, until he catches sight of Indy's conspiratorial wink.

Alabaster dome
of Pankot Palace

Indy and Short
Round's suite

Ceremonial staircase used
by priests and devotees
to access old and
new temples

Secondary
escape route

Willie's luxurious suite
with tunnel access

Giant insects thrive in tunnels

Spike room

Old lava tunnel with stalagmites

Secret route to Temple

Temple of Doom

Crevasse of sacrifice

Walls of volcanic vents
are studded with quartz
and feldspar

Deaths resulting from
dehydration and heat stroke
are common in suffocating
mining areas

Site where first diamonds
were discovered

Water cistern

Extruded rock underlies
mound vegetation

Scrolls housed in anterooms
of old temple contain
accounts and tallies of
Thuggee murder victims

Depleted mining area

Portion of old temple
complex used in the 1830s

Plutonic igneous rock with
some crystallization
supports palace complex

The pair of missing
Sankara Stones

Children sleep
and eat here

Magma reservoir

1 *THUGGEE HIGH PRIEST* Mola
Ram delights in the idea of having a
great archaeologist under his control.
Bent backward over a hideous statue,
the priest's victim is forced to gulp the
bitter blood of Kali Ma.

PANKOT

KNOWN SINCE ANCIENT TIMES as the "wounded" or "bleeding" mount, Pankot rises from a tropical valley dotted with pools of scalding water and cave systems reeking of sulfurous fumes—a perfect setting for wickedness. Magma originating 124 miles (200 km) below the surface has belched fossils and precious stones into the mount's internal labyrinth of volcanic vents. Over the centuries the natural tunnels have been enlarged and linked, and vast subterranean caverns have become sites for the enactment of covert rituals. When garnets, then diamonds were discovered, the gemstones funded construction of the sprawling pleasure palace that exists today, and has served the needs of generations of Maharajahs.

2 MOLA RAM is satisfied that Dr. Jones is deep in the black sleep of Kali Ma when he willingly assists in lowering his blonde consort into the magma pit. Kali is sure to appreciate the offering of such an exotic sacrifice.

3 SPEEDING ON parallel tracks, the pair of mine cars are all but touching when Short Round becomes the object of a tug-of-war between Thuggee guards and the escaping Westerners.

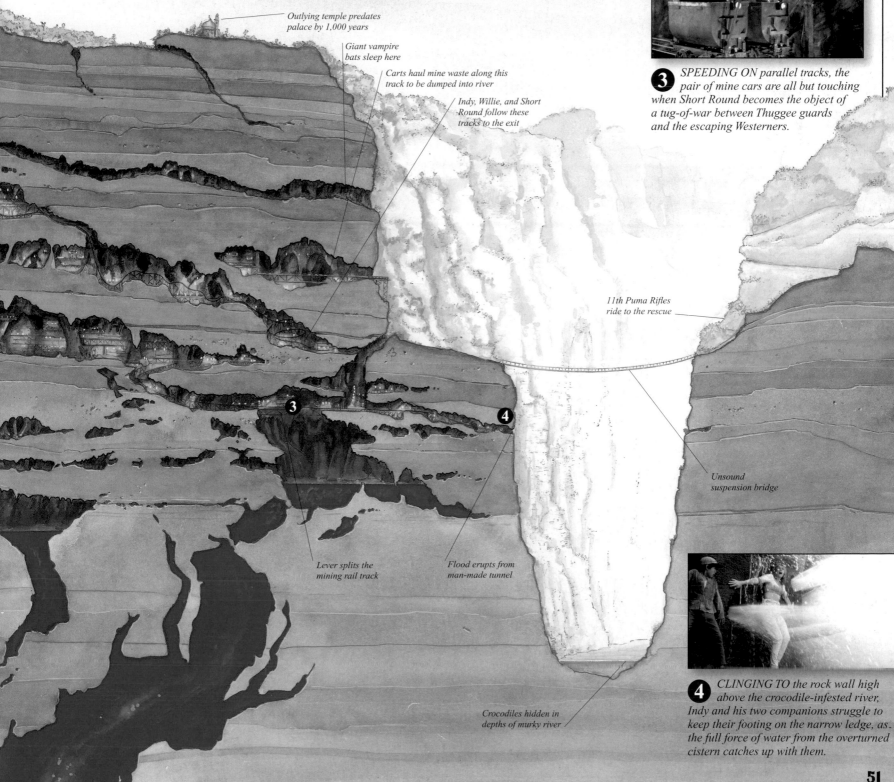

Outlying temple predates palace by 1,000 years

Giant vampire bats sleep here

Carts haul mine waste along this track to be dumped into river

Indy, Willie, and Short Round follow these tracks to the exit

11th Puma Rifles ride to the rescue

Unsound suspension bridge

Lever splits the mining rail track

Flood erupts from man-made tunnel

Crocodiles hidden in depths of murky river

4 CLINGING TO the rock wall high above the crocodile-infested river, Indy and his two companions struggle to keep their footing on the narrow ledge, as the full force of water from the overturned cistern catches up with them.

BID FOR FREEDOM

EAST OF THE PALACE, a hundred-meter-deep gorge has been etched into the landscape by a river that tumbles from the towering mountains surrounding Pankot Province. For centuries the gorge served to defend the palace from marauding groups. But during the decades that the Thuggee used Pankot as a headquarters, a suspension bridge was constructed to span the chasm, shortening the journey from New Delhi and other centers. The bridge fell into disrepair during the reign of Zalim Singh's father, Premjit, and is now used only in extreme circumstances, and only by the bravest or most desperate of travelers. Having taken the three Sankara Stones from the Thuggee temple, it looks like the bridge will have to be Indy's route out of Pankot.

A CRUSHING BLOW

Even with the Sankara Stones tucked safely into his trusty satchel and Willie and Short Round by his side, Indy isn't going anywhere without the children Mola Ram has imprisoned to do his dirty work. Unfortunately for Jones, the biggest and meanest of the Thuggee guards has other plans for him. Seriously outmatched and at times rendered powerless by Zalim Singh's stabbing attacks on the krtya doll, Indy is ultimately hurled onto a conveyor belt of a rock-crushing device. Short Round knocks the krtya doll from Zalim's hands and the guard ends up flattened, notwithstanding Indiana's generous last-minute attempts to rescue him.

THRILL RIDE

In the wake of the children's mad dash for freedom, Mola Ram and his guards have sealed off all exits to the palace. Indy, Willie, and Short Round's only means of escape is a mine car used to haul pulverized rock from the work areas. Brought out of the sleep of Kali Ma by quick-thinking Short Round, Zalim Singh has directed them to take the left fork in the tracks. However, missing the turn, they are swept into a roller-coaster pursuit through winding tunnels and over magma-filled abysses.

FINAL TOLL

Indy emerges from the mine and races for the suspension bridge, minutes behind Willie and Short Round. Just when the coast looks clear, a pair of Thuggee guards intercepts him. The blades of their sabers gleam in the sunlight, but Indiana knows they are no match for his revolver. When his gun hand slaps an empty holster, however, Indy's smug smile vanishes. Falling back on his fighting skills, he forces the guards to duel each other before driving them off with his bullwhip.

SUPPERTIME

The river crocodiles have grown accustomed to receiving grisly meals, thrown to them from the suspension bridge. Fully-clothed humans are a novelty, but pose no problem for the crocodiles' powerful jaws.

Elaborate headcloths, eyeliner, and face paint were introduced to the Thugee cult by Mola Ram.

DIVIDE AND CONQUER

Lao Che had promised Indy that he would soon be joining Wu Han in the Great Unknown, and Indy is beginning to believe him. Trapped on the rickety suspension bridge between groups of advancing guards, Dr. Jones sets the honed edge of a Thuggee sword against one of the frayed rope cables. Warning Short Round in Mandarin, he secures himself to the bridge and severs the cable, expecting the bridge to overturn, but he is surprised when it collapses in half.

HOT POTATO

Mola Ram and Indy engage in a tug-of-war for possession of the satchel that holds the Sankara Stones. Indy intones the Sanskrit warning he read on the wall of the chamber in Willie's bedroom and the stones catch fire. When one of them slips from the satchel, it lands like a live coal in Ram's hand—and he plunges to his death among the crocodiles.

IN THE NICK OF TIME

Contrary to what the villagers of Mayapore believed, the authorities were paying attention to their plight. In fact, Captain Blumburtt's surprise visit to Pankot Palace was not part of a simple inspection tour. Just in time, members of the 11th Puma Rifles arrive at the suspension bridge to open fire on Thuggee archers who are sending flights of arrows against Indy.

Indy is as skillful with a saber as he is with a whip or pistol —and just as dangerous.

Convinced she wants nothing further to do with Indy, Willie quickly changes her mind as Dr. Jones takes her in his arms. However, their romantic moment is abruptly interrupted by a swarm of grateful children and a dousing from Short Round's baby elephant!

RAIDERS OF
THE LOST ARK (1936)

IT IS THE PAST that catches up with Indiana Jones when he agrees to assist
the United States government in preventing the Nazis from acquiring the
Ark of the Covenant—a chest believed to contain the fragments of the
original Ten Commandments tablets. Indy's first task is to track down a
former mentor, who had left the country ten years earlier. This mission also
reunites him with his arch-rival, a mercenary treasure-hunter who has
undermined Indy in the past and is now working for the Nazis. Then there is
the Ark—the mysterious contents of which had changed the course of
human history in the distant past and has the ability to do so again. The
quest takes Indy on an international journey from the college in Connecticut
that employs him as a professor, to mountainous Nepal, to an archaeological
dig in Egypt, and, finally, to a Mediterranean island the Nazis have
converted into a secret submarine base. It is here that the destinies of
everyone involved will be altered—forever.

QUEST FOR THE ARK

THE QUESTS FOR THE CHACHAPOYAN FERTILITY IDOL and the Ark of the Covenant take Indiana Jones to a dozen locations on five continents, and find him riding a horse one day and a U-boat the next. He flies in two seaplanes—one a simple barnstormer; the other, a so-called flying boat. He travels in cars, trucks, and a rundown freighter. And he has at least passing contact with llamas, mules, snakes, yaks, monkeys, camels, and a variety of Amazonian insects and Mediterranean fish. By the time Indy returns to the United States, he has circumnavigated the globe.

NEVADA DESERT

Linked to California by US Highway 91, southern Nevada boasts one of the wonders of the modern world: Boulder Dam, completed last year (1935). Lesser-known wonders exist on the edges of the dry salt flat known as Groom Lake, including test flight areas for the B-17 Flying Fortress, secret-project development labs at Nellis Air Force Base, and storage warehouses that don't appear on public maps.

PAN AM CLIPPER

Inaugurated in 1936, Pan Am Airways' "China Clipper" service between San Francisco's Alameda Seaplane Base and Manila, the Philippines—a distance of 8200 air miles (13,194 km)—takes 60 hours, spread out over five days. Although the luxurious Martin M-130 flying boat has seats for 46, most flights carry only a dozen passengers, all of whom have shelled out close to $1,000 for one-way tickets. Flying unpressurized at 8,000 feet (2,438 m), the plane is noisy, but Pullman bunks are available for those who can pull down their hat brims and fall asleep anywhere.

PACIFIC OCEAN

HANGAR 51, NEVADA DESERT

SAN FRANCISCO, USA

To KATHMANDU, NEPAL

WAKE ISLAND

MANILA, PHILIPPINES

HAWAII

CHACHAPOYAS

Defined by the confluences of the Marañón, Utcubamba, and Bagua Rivers, the Chachapoyas region is often draped with low-hanging clouds that nourish the thick vegetation of the sierra. This "eyebrow of the forest" is home to the ruins of ancient ceremonial centers and strategically located funerary statues and sarcophagi, some of which were seen by early Spanish explorers; many of them remain to be re-discovered.

KEY

1. *Losing the Golden Idol to Belloq in Chachapoyas, Indy returns to the US via Manaus*
2. *Now working for the US government, Dr. Jones flies from New York to San Francisco*
3. *In search of Abner Ravenwood, Indy boards the China Clipper for the Philippines*
4. *Indy flies from Manila to Calcutta to Kathmandu; from there he drives to Patan*
5. *Air East Asia takes Indy and Marion to the Middle East; from Bagdad they fly to Cairo*
6. *From Cairo, Indy, Marion and the Ark reach the Med aboard the freighter* Bantu Wind
7. *Jones clings to a U-boat periscope to reach the sub pen on the secret Nazi island*
8. *A fishing boat carries Indy and Marion to Athens, from where they fly to Washington, D.C.*
9. *The Ark makes a lonely journey by rail to a warehouse in southern Nevada*

GERMAN U-BOAT

The Treaty of Versailles (1919) prohibited Germany from building submarines. But the Third Reich found a way around the proviso by classifying *unterseeboot* (U-boat) construction as "research," which was permitted. Designed to enforce naval blockades and fire on merchant vessels, the new class of subs can spend longer periods of time underwater, but stick to the surface, submerging only when necessary. Submarine pens, like those at *Geheimhaven* base, north of Crete, are reinforced to withstand aerial bombardment.

MARSHALL COLLEGE, Conn.

Founded in the early 1700s as a prep school, Marshall received a collegiate charter in 1853 and was named for the generosity of its chief patron, Frederic Marshall. A private liberal arts college, Marshall is famous for its literature, linguistics, and archaeology departments. A branch of New York's National Museum, which Dr. Marcus Brody oversees, sits on campus.

HIMALAYA MOUNTAINS

With a name derived from the Nepalese word himal, meaning "snow-covered mountain," the Himalaya—thrust upward by the collision of continental plates—is among Earth's youngest ranges. Everest has yet to be scaled, and has already claimed the lives of George Mallory and Andrew Irvine. But a route to the summit has just been found by Bill Tilman and Eric Shipton.

PATAN

Lalitpur—as many of the elder locals insist on calling Patan—lies near Kathamandu. Thought to have been laid out to mimic the Buddhist Wheel of Righteousness, the city is embraced by four sacred mounds that rise from the cardinal points. The Raven Tavern is close to the center, a stone's throw from Durbar Square, where kids offer to clean the wax from your ears for a few rupiah.

2 MARSHALL COLLEGE, USA
NEW YORK CITY, USA

WASHINGTON, D.C., USA

ATHENS, GREECE

8

SECRET NAZI ISLAND NEAR CRETE

7

6 TANIS, NILE DELTA

BAGHDAD, IRAQ

KATHMANDU, NEPAL

PATAN, NEPAL

ATLANTIC OCEAN

MEDITERRANEAN SEA

CAIRO, EGYPT

5

KARACHI, PAKISTAN

1

MANAUS, BRAZIL

CHACHAPOYAS, PERU

OLD QUARTER, Cairo

Incorporated into the city of Cairo, the old bazaars and trader's inns of Fustat comprise the heart of Cairo's Old Quarter. Founded when a dove laid an egg in the tent of Arab military commander 'Amr ibn al-'As, Fustat remained a "town of tents" until the building of the stately mosques that now sit next to synagogues and Coptic churches.

TANIS, Nile Delta

The desert sands shift and the pedestal base of an ancient pot is uncovered. Scooped up by a trader from Tunisia, the piece is brought to the village of San el-Hagar, and sold to an Egyptian whose shop has many such pieces, and which is often visited by rich Europeans with a taste for antiquities. Perhaps the found pot comes from the ruins of Tanis.

SEARCH FOR THE GOLDEN IDOL

RUMORS OF AN ANCIENT CHACHAPOYAN TEMPLE yet to be plundered by treasure-hunters had circulated in archaeological circles for fifty years. The Peruvian site was said to be located close to a lonely summit known locally as El Panal—the Bee-Hive—and a dangerous cataract called "Dead Man Falls." Now Indy has a map—part of one, at any rate: a centuries-old piece of parchment that details some of the route to the temple. More importantly, he has the will to succeed where so many others have failed.

A headdressed, hollow-mouthed demon is one of the markers Indy has been looking for.

AMERICAN IDOL

When a score of golden Chachapoyan figurines begin to appear on the antiquities market, Indy and Marcus Brody, curator of the National Museum, believe that new Chachapoyan temples have been located and are being plundered. All evidence points to one of Indy's competitors, a Princeton archaeologist named Forrestal, who had embarked on an expedition to Peru a year earlier and had yet to return. With help from the journal of a 19th-century explorer and contacts in South America, Indy decides to follow in Forrestal's footsteps, determined to acquire the real prize: a golden representation of the Chachapoyan goddess of fertility and childbirth, said to be secreted in the heart of the Temple of the Warriors.

Indy joins gazes with the snarling idol, steeling himself for the swap.

RIVER ROGUES

A fragment of the parchment map is known to be in the calloused hands of two cutthroat Peruvian guides, Satipo and Barranca, whose chief haunt is a rum-soaked Amazonian river landing called Machete Junction. Indy is aware that the pair has used their map to lure guileless explorers to their deaths, but he makes a deal with them anyway, as their portion of the map is essential to locating the hidden temple.

Barranca learns the hard way that Indiana Jones isn't just another dupe, when Indy's bullwhip lashes around his gun hand before he can fire. Fleeing into the jungle, Barranca doesn't realize that he's scurrying to a worse fate: a swarm of poison-tipped blowgun darts loosed by a band of Chachapoyan warriors called the Hovitos.

INDY SWEEPS THE WHIP IN AN ENCIRCLING ARC. AND SUDDENLY...

BLAM!

A POINTED EXCHANGE

A short distance into the cave-like corridor that accesses the temple, Indy and Satipo discover where Forrestal met his end. Having broken a beam of skewed sunlight, Indy's competitor had tripped a bed of wooden spikes that shot out from the wall of the tunnel, impaling him. The deadly spikes are only one in a series of traps Indy and Satipo must negotiate to reach the temple rotunda. A pity that Satipo didn't pay better attention on the way in—he might have avoided being impaled on the way out.

ROLLING THUNDER

If only he had emptied the pouch of two handfuls of sand before swapping it for the Golden Idol, Indy berates himself as he races from the collapsing temple. Pressure-sensitive, the disk that the idol sat upon has descended into the plinth, setting off a cataclysmic chain-reaction. Indy wonders if he's going to pay for his overconfidence by being flattened by a boulder or sealed inside the temple. Either way, it looks as if the ancient Chachapoyans may have the last laugh.

"Too bad the Hovitos don't know you the way I do, Belloq."
—Indiana Jones

DRESSED FOR SUCCESS

In fact, the one to have the last laugh is a charming mercenary named René Belloq, who is waiting outside the temple with a band of Hovitos at his back to relieve Indy of the idol that has already cost so many lives. Indy's arch-rival in the antiquity trade for more than a decade, Belloq likes to remind Indy at every opportunity that there is nothing Indy can possess that Belloq cannot take from him.

Former stunt pilot and loyal Yankees fan, Jock Lindsey, had been figuring on a couple of days of fishing while Indy explored. Instead, Jock, Indy, and Jock's pet snake, Reggie, are forced to execute an emergency take-off out of the jungle.

THE GOLD GODDESS

Years later, Indy regains the idol from a dealer in black market antiquities in Marrakesh, Morocco. However, also on the trail of the idol is Xomec, a descendant of the Chachapoyans, and Ilsa Toht, sister of Gestapo agent Arnold Toht. The two want to use the idol to unite Amazonian tribes and disrupt wartime rubber production in South America, as well as lure Indy to his death.

TEMPLE TRAIL

THE LOCATION OF the Temple of the Warriors is a secret to all but high priests and clan leaders. The temple houses the most venerated of the Chachapoyan deities, the Earth mother and fertility goddess whom the Inca would call Pachamama and whose image is embodied in a small, snarling golden idol that sits at the heart of the structure. A series of traps and snares tested the skill of fledgling Chachapoyan soldiers, who had to work their way to the idol, touch her, and depart. Survival conferred worthiness and the right to wear the scarlet macaw feathers of a warrior. Now it is Indy's turn.

1 *ARRIVING AT THE RIVER, Dr. Jones joins his pieces of the parchment map scraps to the piece the guides have been using to lure unwary travelers to their deaths.*

5

Pellucid pool

Dead Man Falls

1

Eight-foot-tall Chachapoyan demon idol houses bird nests

Ancient broken pottery

Underpinnings of an ancient road that crossed the Andes Mountains

A second statue, not shown on the map, lies concealed in rubble

Old outer-wall construction eroded by semi-annual flooding of river

Piranhas and highly venomous snakes make this a deadly crossing

After studying the reunited map, Indy uses his whip to send Barranca fleeing for his life

3 *INDY IS REUNITED with his competitor for archaeological treasures, Dr. Forrestal. Forrestal met his fate by stepping into a beam of sunlight, activating a spring-loaded rack of spears.*

4 *MOST OF the truncated diamond-shaped floor stones are linked to tubes concealed in the walls that fire poison-tipped darts across the temple rotunda.*

2 *SATIPO IS RELUCTANT* to follow Indy into the dark passageway, for it is said that no one who has entered the temple has ever been seen again.

Shaft of sunlight cannot be broken without activating spears from the crossbow

Boulder is released by a simple lever acting on a hidden wedge

Indy's bullwhip takes him and Satipo across chasm

Prismatic crystal directs and intensifies beam of light

Door closes when wedge under idol plinth is removed

Stone wedges come out of the wall, causing the temple structure to collapse, when Indy removes the idol

Golden fertility idol is the exact weight to hold the ancient self-destruct mechanism in place

Belloq, a band of Hovitos, and the dart-skewered body of Barranca wait for Indy

Precision stonework, without mortar, was perfected by Incan masons

Sloped tunnel curves behind the temple rotunda

Ancient burial chambers of older temples, deliberately buried beneath the Temple of Warriors

Core of temple is empty to allow building to collapse when trap is set off

Satipo waits for Indy at golden Sun circle

Bellows, operated by levers and weights, trigger flights of poison-tipped darts

Carved head left over from an earlier civilization

Ancient daykeeper interred in traditional sitting posture

5 *STEPS AHEAD* of a band of Hovitos warriors armed with spears, blowguns, and bow and arrows, Jones races back toward the lake tributary where Indy's friend Jock has landed his biplane.

MARCUS BRODY

THOUGH HE HAS SPENT MOST OF HIS LIFE in the United States, Marcus Brody has retained traces of his native British accent, and on most occasions, prefers a bowler hat to a fedora. A graduate of Oxford, where he met and became fast friends with Henry Jones Sr., Marcus did fieldwork in North American archaeology before becoming assistant curator of the National Museum in 1913. After losing his wife to pneumonia, Marcus devoted himself completely to the museum, honing his talent for dealing with harried accountants and acquisitive contributors alike. As a favor, Marcus took Henry's spirited thirteen-year-old son on a field trip to Egypt. Years later, Indy would repay the favor by helping to track down Marcus's brother-in-law, who'd gone missing in Chile.

CLOSE FRIENDS

Witness to Indy's estrangement from Henry, Marcus judges neither of them. He helps bolster Indy's taste for the good life by dispatching him on missions more appropriate for a curator than an archaeologist, and accepts without question the artifacts Indy acquires in the field. A surrogate father, he thinks of Indy as a light in the darkness and a man of idiosyncratic convictions.

SCHOLARS AND SPIES

Marcus is as excited as Indy is to learn from Agents Musgrove and Eaton of the discovery of Tanis, Egypt, where it is believed the Ark of the Covenant lies. The prospect of beating the Nazis to the Ark is more reason for celebration. Five years earlier Marcus might even have gone after the Ark himself. But while the fabled chest represents everything that drew Indy and Marcus to archaeology to begin with, the search is not something to be taken lightly. Moreover, Marcus knows that renewed contact with Abner Ravenwood, who holds an important clue as to the whereabouts of the Ark, and his daughter, Marion, is likely to take an emotional toll on Indy.

TOUGH GUY

In 1936, Marcus joins Indy and Marion on a mission to Wales to track down a notorious Arab smuggler. There, Marcus encounters an old college pal named Austin "Cutter" Coleridge, who has been excavating a site known as Lucifer's Chamber, which is believed to be a gateway to a city of gold. When Marcus is taken prisoner, he shows his old chum that he is still good with his fists, even though it is thirty years since he won the bantam-weight title at Princeton University.

Indy and Marcus have a history of working together to acquire artifacts, going back to their discovery of the Ring of Osiris in 1913. But Marcus knows that antiquities are not always easily prized from the ruins where they are found.

When a weary Marcus has to travel to Iskenderun alone, Indy is concerned. He knows that Marcus—who only speaks English and ancient Greek and once got lost in the National Museum archive rooms—is a fretful traveler, but trusts that his friend Sallah will take good care of him.

"At my age, I'm prepared to take a few things on faith."
—Marcus Brody

Marcus sometimes regrets that he has become an academician and armchair adventurer, and secretly yearns to get back in the saddle.

TWO PEAS IN A POD

Marcus's caring relationship with Indy is in large measure the product of his long-standing affection for Henry, who frequently shares his son's penchant for getting in over his head. Six years Henry's junior, Marcus looked up to the Scotsman at Oxford, and forty years later still remembers their university club toasts to the "genius of the Restoration," replete with missed handshakes, ritual arm flaps, and ear-tugging.

THE VOICE OF REASON

Even when smiling, Marcus looks vaguely apprehensive, especially when he is out of his element, away from the museum. Even a trip to Venice seems daunting until he is assured that lodging has already been arranged. And at Iskenderun, after rejecting offers of water—because fish make love in it—and chickens—because he is a vegetarian—Marcus is quick to tell Sallah not to panic, and that everything is under control.

HEAD AND SHOULDERS ABOVE THE REST

In 1939, Marcus retired as curator of the National Museum to accept a position as Dean of Students at Marshall College, a post he held until 1944. The career change meant fewer honorariums for Indy, but resulted in the forging of an even deeper friendship between the two men. Marcus's passing in 1952 nearly derailed Indiana, who lobbied hard for the bronze statue that has adorned the Marshall campus ever since. Indy likes to think that the statue watches closely over him and his work.

Lost in the swirl of activity, Marcus wonders what in the world he is doing in Iskenderun.

MARION RAVENWOOD

A PLUCKY, FRECKLE-FACED FIREBRAND some ten years younger than Indy, Marion is the only child of an academic father, Abner Ravenwood, who was obsessed with myth, the search for fabled antiquities, and, especially, the Ark of the Covenant. The quest for clues to its whereabouts not only took him all over the world, but led to the loss of his professorship at the University of Chicago, and a decade of hard-won travels through the Middle East and Asia, with Marion begrudgingly accompanying him nearly every step of the way. Their hardscrabble existence dashed many of Marion's girlhood dreams, but also gave rise to a capricious spirit.

Marion frequently engages unsuspecting patrons of The Raven in drinking contests as a means of supplementing her earnings.

PROPRIETOR OF THE RAVEN

Effectively stranded in Patan, Nepal, after Abner's death in an avalanche, Marion ekes out an existence by continuing to operate a ramshackle tavern. The Raven Tavern caters to a rough local crowd, as well as to groups of seasoned mountain climbers, their Sherpas, and porters en route to ascents in the Himalayas, but the spirited Marion is more than capable of holding her own. However, bluster gets Marion only so far when a sadistic Gestapo officer turns up at The Raven with treasures on his mind.

> *"Indiana Jones. Always knew someday you'd come walking back through my door."*
> —Marion Ravenwood

A TWO-FISTED WELCOME

Like a bad penny, Indiana Jones—the most gifted bum Abner ever trained—just keeps turning up. Marion has learned to hate him in the past ten years, for dating and ditching her when she was just a teenager, but more for failing to rescue her from the grueling, nomadic life Abner dragged her into. Indy may not have meant to hurt her, but *she* means to hurt him now, welcoming him with a rueful smile and a powerful punch across the jaw.

The medallion is inscribed with ancient characters and adorned with a red crystal.

THE VALUE OF MEMORY

Marion has sold off most of Abner's collection of archaeological finds, but she has kept one treasure for sentimental, as well as practical reasons. A bronze medallion, it is the headpiece of an ancient Egyptian staff Abner believed could pinpoint the resting place of the Ark of the Covenant, should the lost city of Tanis ever be discovered.

Memories of Marion's late father flooded in as Marion gazes at his most prized possession.

IT'S TIME I STARTED CALLING THE SHOTS IN THIS RELATIONSHIP.

AND LEAVE THE MONEY HERE.

PAYBACK TIME

Indy claims to be sorry for abandoning Marion, and she takes bitter delight in hearing him say it. But everybody has something to be sorry about.
She orders him to return the following day, but sweetens the command with a kiss. The fact that he labels the medallion worthless and then offers five grand for it assures her there's even more to be had. And she means to milk every penny out of him, if only in repayment for his ruining her life.

No stranger to street fights and bar brawls, Marion shows herself to be a gutsy combatant when she and Indy are set upon by knife-wielding assailants in a Cairo bazaar.

ALL DRESSED UP

Marion is not above using her looks and her wiles to her advantage. Captured by the Nazis and brought to the Tanis archaeological dig, she flirts openly with French mercenary René Belloq, agreeing to wear the dress he has procured for her, and hoping to drink him under the table.

FURTHER ADVENTURES

Marion later opens a swanky version of The Raven in New York, but the club fails. When the chance arises for her to relocate to London, she jumps at it, remaining there for some time after she and Indy part ways.

Indy's down-payment on Marion's brighter future

REUNITED

Partners, for a time after the Ark has been found and lost once more, Marion and Indy face off against a Nazi named Vogel in West Africa. They also investigate rumors that Abner is still alive, in an adventure that takes them to a hidden city in the Himalayan Mountains.

EGYPT

ARRIVING IN CAIRO, EGYPT, Indiana and Marion seek out Indy's longtime friend and frequent accomplice, Sallah Mohammed Faisel el-Kahir. A noted guide and project manager for archaeological excavations, Sallah brings Indy up to speed on what has been transpiring at the Tanis dig, for which the Germans have hired every strong back in Egypt. Regardless, the Ark of the Covenant has continued to elude them, despite the presence of a French archaeologist Indy quickly identifies as none other than René Belloq. Still, Indy feels certain that even his arch-rival will fail at locating the Well of Souls without access to the headpiece of the Staff of Ra.

Decades earlier, Sallah helped Indy and Marcus Brody locate an ancient ring and escape an outbreak of bubonic plague.

THEIR FIRST BABY

Marion grows attached to a Capuchin monkey sporting a red vest that shows up unannounced at Sallah's crowded house. She thinks the monkey has Indy's looks, and he thinks it has her brains. Indeed, the monkey is cleverer than it looks and acts as a spotter for its handler: an eyepatched Arab assassin dressed in a bedraggled djellaba.

A BIG HEART

Named for the builder of Cairo's Citadel, Salah al-Din, jovial Sallah lives in Cairo's Old Quarter with his wife, Fayah, and their brood of children. After parenthood and archaeology, opera is his passion, and his rich baritone voice often fills the local bazaars with the strains of Gilbert and Sullivan songs. He is among the few to understand that the Ark is not of this Earth, and is meant to remain hidden. Loyal to a fault, he helps Indy find it anyway.

OTHER ADVENTURES WITH SALLAH

Accompanying Indy to Marrakesh, Morocco in 1937, Sallah uses his strong back to lower Indy into a treasure trove. The trove is owned by Saad Hassim, a dealer in black market antiquities who purchased the golden Chachapoyan fertility idol from René Belloq.

> I LOVE THIS LIFE, INDY! LOVE IT!

> OHHH, SING AWAY YE WINDS OF HEAVEN, WAFTING HIGH O'ER CHARON'S BROW...

Marion hides from the Nazis in a basket, which is quickly loaded onto the back of a truck.

Indy finds solace in a bottle of cheap drink. Bad enough that he had run roughshod over Marion's heart, he now believes he is responsible for her death. His grief deepens when even the monkey seems to cry out for her. Sallah tries to tell Indy that life goes on, but for Indy nothing will ever be the same again.

MARION!

MARION!

NOT IN THE PLAN

As Marion is bundled into the truck, her call for help echoes in the bazaar's narrow alleyways. Indy gives chase, frightening stray cats, angering and amusing merchants, dodging machine-gun fire, flinging coins to insistent beggars, and overturning baskets in a frantic search. Shooting the driver of the munitions-laden truck he thinks contains Marion, he watches in horror as the vehicle goes out of control and explodes.

A series of fights break out in the bazaar square between Indy and scimitar-wielding assailants.

A SHADOWY REFLECTION

Belloq wants to convince Indy, in a civilized way, that they are not as unlike as Indy wishes to believe. Both have fallen from the religion they have made of archaeology—the pure light of the quest. When Belloq confesses his plan to speak with God by means of the Ark of the Covenant, Indy, with little left to live for, is eager to facilitate Belloq's plan, by killing him on the spot.

CRACKING THE CODE

Rescued by Sallah's children from the forced encounter with Belloq, Indy meets with an astrologer who deciphers the glyphs etched into the perimeter of Marion's medallion. With the night air riotous with the sound of cicadas, Indy and Sallah grasp that Belloq and the Nazis are digging for the Ark of the Covenant in the wrong place. Meanwhile, the monkey's handler has poisoned some dates waiting to be enjoyed.

Feeling dead on his feet, Indy draws his gun and shoots with weary casualness.

First to the dates, the Capuchin receives its just reward. Snatching from mid-air a date Indy tosses, Sallah saves him from a similar fate.

RENÉ BELLOQ

BORN INTO WEALTH at the Forteresse Malevil in Marseilles, René Emile Belloq grew up admiring France's most celebrated archaeologists, eventually enrolling in the Sorbonne with an eye toward following in their footsteps. Ambitious and competitive from the start, Belloq won the Archaeology Society Prize for a paper on stratigraphy, which was later revealed to contain passages "borrowed" from a similar paper written by fellow student Indiana Jones. Nevertheless, the prize, along with financial contributions from his family, helped Belloq land an assistant curator's position at the Louvre, which he held until his darker side revealed itself again.

CLOSE ENCOUNTERS

In 1934, two years before making off with the Chachapoyan idol, Belloq's contacts in the antiquities trade had told him that Indy had discovered the location of an unexcavated site in Saudi Arabia. Arriving in Rub' al Khali just days ahead of Jones, Belloq absconded with various artifacts left by a long-vanished nomadic group. Even earlier, Belloq had repeatedly foiled Indy's attempts to regain an allegedly cursed crystal skull Indy had unearthed in Cozan, British Honduras.

FROM CURATOR TO MERCENARY

Less than a year into his job at the Louvre, Belloq was accused of having financed the looting of a site in Persia that resulted in the deaths of several museum employees and a British archaeologist. With the theft of artifacts uncovered in the royal tombs of Ur, in Iraq, he made a name for himself with the dealers of black market antiquities and the private collectors that were their clients. Fired from his museum position, Belloq became more amoral, hiring his talents out to the highest bidders.

THE COMPANY HE KEEPS

Tasked with keeping Belloq under rein, Colonel Dietrich and his aide, Gobler, have little interest in the Ark beyond acquiring it for Hitler. But Gestapo agent Arnold Toht has even less interest. Initially assigned to shadow Indy, the nearsighted agent with the sinister whisper, sadist's smile, and swastika lapel pin, relishes each and every opportunity to inflict pain on his adversaries. Even the folding hanger for his leather coat resembles an instrument of torture.

CHANCE OF A LIFETIME

Where Belloq had once courted fame, he now contents himself with power. And so he sees no problem in collaborating with the Nazis when it serves his purpose—this, despite the fact that the captain of a German U-boat had double-crossed him and destroyed Forteresse Malevil with two well-placed torpedoes. When Colonel Herman Dietrich seeks him out to assist in locating the Ark of the Covenant, Belloq recognizes it as a chance to achieve ultimate power.

VILLAIN AND HERO

Over the years, Belloq has tried to coax Indy to join him in the shadowy realm he inhabits, sometimes going so far as to furnish him with rumors of new finds and information on rivals. Following Marion's disappearance, Belloq attempts to explain one last time that he and Indy are but opposite sides of the same coin. Though he has already tried to kill Indy in Peru, and surely means to have him killed now, Belloq laments the loss of a worthy adversary.

Calling Indy's bluff to destroy the Ark with a grenade, Belloq proves that he was right about what he told Indy in Cairo: archaeology has become Indy's religion.

A MAN OF TASTE

Belloq assures Dietrich that Marion knows nothing about the Staff of Ra headpiece, but just to be sure he wants to interrogate her before Toht gets the chance. Drinking together, they talk about everything but the headpiece. In fact, Belloq is attracted to Marion, and briefly wishes the Nazis would disappear.

"Jones, your persistence surprises even me."
—René Belloq

UNCOVERING THE TRUTH

When the Ark is located, Belloq ignores Dietrich's misgivings about performing a "Jewish ritual," and has the Ark carried to a natural amphitheater. More a true believer than Indy, Belloq will do whatever it takes to unlock the mysteries of the universe. Attired in garments designed according to instructions given in the Old Testament and reciting Aramaic incantations, Belloq attempts to summon the truth into the open.

Gazing into the opened Ark, Belloq whispers, "Reveal to me the secrets of existence."

THE WELL OF SOULS

THOUSANDS OF YEARS AGO, King Shishaq's dream-interpreter, Userhet, advised that the stolen Ark of the Covenant had to be hidden from the view of the mistrustful sun god, Amun-Ra. Shishaq had the sacred coffer interred in a building known as the Well of Souls in Tanis, Egypt. He ordered the construction of a special Map Room that would allow Amun-Ra to perpetually monitor the Ark's whereabouts. But Shishaq's actions were no protection against the wrath of the Israelite's god. A year after the Ark was placed in its sanctuary, a sandstorm of epic proportions buried the entire city of Tanis, and the location of the Well of Souls was seemingly lost to history—until Indiana Jones appeared on the scene, that is.

In the Map Room, Indy inserts his staff into the calendar tablet. At just after nine a.m., sunlight strikes the headpiece crystal, illuminating the location of the Well of Souls in the city replica.

THE STUFF OF DREAMS

The upraised arms of a quartet of colossal Anubis statues support the ceiling of the Well of Souls. Approached by a short flight of steps at the far end of the rectangular chamber is an altar stone, atop which rests a large stone chest, similar to a sarcophagus and etched with hieroglyphics that recount Shishaq's story. Inside the box, Indy and Sallah find the Ark, which is made of gilded acacia wood and adorned with an elaborate crown and two winged cherubs with heads bowed in reverence. Sallah is not enthusiastic about moving the Ark, but he's willing to make any sacrifice for his American friend.

Indy, Sallah, and ten diggers ascend the mound and work through the day and night to locate an entrance to the Well of Souls. Meanwhile, ominous clouds gather in the southern sky, and bolts of lightning stab the arid landscape.

Indy is stunned to stumble on Marion, bound and gagged in Belloq's tent. But as relieved as he is to find her alive, rescuing her might prompt the Germans to search the ruins high and low, and the Ark must be secured beforehand.

THE SNAKE PIT

To reach the Ark, Indy and Sallah must first deal with thousands of asps, cobras, and other snakes that blanket the floor. For Indy, this makes the Well of Souls a true hell on earth. Spraying the snakes with kerosene he brought along to fuel the torches, Indy carefully threads his way through the serpents.

The voice of God spoke to Moses from between the cherubim.

The Ark is believed to contain the Staff of Aaron.

Indy fights back an urge to lift the lid of the Ark, which seems to glow from within.

...AND BEFORE INDY'S HORRIFIED EYES, *MARION* PLUNGES INTO THE WELL OF SOULS!

NOOOOOooo!

ADIEU, DR. JONES

When Belloq observes a group of workers gathered atop an unexcavated mound, he knows at once that Indiana Jones has something to do with it. Backed by a contingent of soldiers, Belloq clambers to the summit, astonished to find the long-sought Ark of the Covenant crated and waiting for him. Much to his dismay, however, Toht unceremoniously hurls Marion into the Well of Souls to join Jones in captivity and slow death.

Anubis's keen canine nose sniffs the dead and escorts only those he finds sweet-smelling and pure.

Symbolic of regeneration and of the night, black is the color the body turns during mummification.

GOOD DOG

Indy thinks there might be a way out of their confinement. With the torches guttering—even those Indy has wrapped with fabric torn from Marion's dress—and the snakes closing in, he uses his whip to scale to the top of one of the Anubis statues. Planting his hands against the ceiling, he rocks the sharp-toothed colossus loose, sending it toppling forward into the far wall of the chamber, and creating an opening into an adjacent room.

"Whatever you're doing, do it faster!"
—Marion Ravenwood

Gloom holds sway as the last of the torches are going out.

Anubis's torso and limbs are human.

An asp Indy stepped on has its sights set on him.

Anubis—the Greek name for the Egyptian god, Anpu—both escorts the dead to the underworld and weighs their hearts against the feather of Ma'at, the goddess of truth.

Wondering where she found the dress, Indy prepares to catch Marion in his arms.

DENIZENS OF THE UNDERWORLD

Marion is so eager to escape the snakes that she hurries through the opening, straight into the arms of a decaying mummy. Scrambling backward, she finds herself pressed in among dozens of the linen-wrapped bodies, some with thick snakes slithering through their gaping jaws. By the time Indy finds her, she is too shaken to comprehend that he has discovered a window to freedom.

TANIS

A RENOWNED CITY OF COMMERCE even before King Shishaq arrived from the Land of the Israelites bearing the Ark of the Covenant, Tanis was strategically located in the Nile delta, and was often referred to as "the northern Thebes." In the nineteenth century, archaeologists Mariette and Flinders carried out initial excavations. Visiting the ruins in the 1920s, Abner Ravenwood unearthed the headpiece to the Staff of Ra close to the village of San el-Hagar, but was unsuccessful in discovering Tanis's Map Room, let alone the Well of Souls.

1 *ATOP THE MAP ROOM mound, Indy, disguised as an Arab worker, prepares to be lowered into the structure by Sallah, who has anchored the rope to a barbwire.*

Supply road links the main road to Cairo

Site of the steed Indy steals to pursue the Ark

Observation/ look-out tower

Indy and Marion's hiding place after the Flying Wing explodes

Communications/ radio mast

Fuel dump

Mess for pilots, mechanics, and communications crew

Fuel truck

Prototype Flying Wing flown in to transport the Ark to Berlin

Windsock

Graded runway

Sand and soil banked up from the creation of a runway and landing circle

Ancient treasure has thus far eluded looters

Thin-walled entrance to treasure trove buried by pre-Shishaq kings

Rubble-filled shaft provides Indy and Marion with an escape route

Catacombs are filled with mummies of royal attendants, packed shoulder to shoulder

Toppled Anubis statue has opened a breach into an adjacent chamber

Guttering torches are no longer a concern to asps and cobras

Snakes wriggle back into the main chamber now that intruders have exited

One of several ancient tunnels explored by looters containing buried ship

Nazi guards supervise the re-burial of the entrance slab

Damaged by tomb-robbers, sarcophagus contains the mummified remains of Shishaq's military commander

2 *TOHT HAS ONLY one side of the Staff of Ra headpiece seared into his palm so the measurement for the staff is incomplete.*

3 *EMERGING FROM THEIR brief imprisonment inside the snake-infested Well of Souls, Indy and Marion gaze out at the Flying Wing, which is meant to carry the Ark of the Covenant to Berlin.*

Mess area
for German
soldiers, where
Indy and Sallah
are nearly
identified

The Map Room
contains a replica
of entire city

René Belloq's
Berber tent, where
he entertains Marion

Storage compound
for food and materials

Indy locates exact position
of Well of Souls from here

Fallen obelisk commemorates Shishaq's
victories in the Land of the Israelites

Track and hoppers for conveying
debris to sifting sites

Head of one of two seated figures
waiting to be unearthed

Partly exposed
sphinx

4 INDY'S PLANS to conceal himself
aboard the Flying Wing go awry
when he is challenged by a German soldier.

Ark waits to be
loaded onto
Flying Wing

Dietrich sometimes
enjoys listening to
Wagner on his
gramophone

LEARNING that the Ark
is on its way to Cairo, **5**
Indy borrows an Arabian
steed and races after it.

RACE FOR THE ARK

DESPITE INDIANA JONES'S EFFORTS at the Flying Wing landing strip, the Ark of the Covenant remains in the hands of archaeologist René Belloq and the Nazis. Never one to surrender, however, Indy tells Sallah and Marion to arrange for transport of the Ark to England—by boat, a plane, or anything! Indiana is uncertain as to just how he is going to regain the Ark and freely admits to making up his plans as he goes along.

1 PACKED INTO a crate emblazoned with Third Reich emblems, the Ark is loaded into the back of a truck bound for Cairo.

2 FINDING TWO Arabian stallions tethered under a canvas shelter close to the landing strip, Indy "borrows" the more compliant of the pair. Heeling the horse in the sides, he gallops off in pursuit of the Ark, while angry Egyptian workers pursue him, waving their fists in the air and cursing him in Arabic.

SPURRING THE STALLION on, Indiana streaks across the sand dunes, making a beeline for the departing Nazi convoy. Racing downhill, he urges the horse to move alongside the speeding truck, then hauls himself aboard, hands grasped on the canvas back and feet planted on the running board. **3**

Once on the side of the truck, Indy throws the passenger out and hurls himself inside.

4 IN A STRUGGLE for control, Indy and the Nazi driver career the truck into a construction site, side-swiping a series of ladders and sending several Arabs flying, one of whom lands on the hood of the truck before jumping off.

5 AWARE THAT Indy has commandeered the truck, soldiers in the back make their way forward on the running boards. Indy succeeds in sending all of them flying, except for one, who crawls across the canvas top and enters the cab.

6 HURLED THROUGH the windshield by the Nazi, Indy tries to hang on to the truck's front grille, the spokes of which begin to bend under the pressure of his weight.

7 WITH THE TRUCK accelerating toward the car that carries Belloq, Dietrich, and Toht, Indiana has to climb down from the front fender and lower himself under the truck.

8 INDY LASHES his whip onto the undercarriage and allows himself to be dragged behind the truck. Then, he begins to inch his way toward the open rear.

9 FROM THE SIDE FLAP of the canvas cover, Indy hooks his hands around the top of the passenger door-frame and throws himself into the cab, kicking the driver from the wheel and tossing him through the windshield.

10 HAVING ALREADY SENT GOBLER and a car-full of Nazis over a towering cliff, Indy uses the truck to nudge Belloq and Dietrich's car to a dusty, grinding halt in the arid wasteland.

11 INDY HURTLES the truck into Omar's garage just before Belloq and others arrive on the scene, to find only a bazaar, bustling with vendors.

12 THE ARK'S ticket out of Egypt is the suspect merchant freighter, Bantu Wind, captained by cigar-smoking Simon Katanga, who relinquishes his personal quarters to Indiana and Marion.

ARRIVAL AT GEHEIMHAVEN

Wise to the arrangements Sallah made with Captain Katanga, the crew aboard the Nazi U-Boat, Wurfler, intercepts the Bantu Wind at sea. Belloq retakes the Ark—and Marion. He refuses to believe that Indy has been killed by the crew and thrown overboard and transfers both the Ark and Marion to the submarine. René is correct: Indiana has swum to the submarine and uses his bullwhip to lash himself to the periscope as the sub enters the Nazi base.

ARK CEREMONY

ON A ROCKY ISLAND off the coast of North Africa, the Nazis have constructed a subterranean supply depot and submarine pen. It is to this location that the Ark of the Covenant is being transported. Determined to rescue Marion, Indiana Jones descends from the conning tower of the Nazi U-Boat, the *Wurrfler*, eases himself into the chill waters of the Mediterranean, and swims ashore. Disguised in a somewhat ill-fitting Nazi uniform, Indy manages to succeed in infiltrating Belloq and Colonel Dietrich's group as they head inland with the Ark of the Covenant.

Armed with a prototype grenade launcher he has discovered among the Nazi arsenal, Indy threatens to destroy the Ark unless Marion is released. Unfortunately, Belloq calls Indy's bluff and he is taken prisoner as well.

BELLOQ'S RITUAL

The Nazi guards follow Belloq up to the altar, carrying the golden Ark.

Dietrich is infuriated by the fact that the detour to the submarine base was arranged in secret by Belloq. The French archaeologist had insisted that opening the Ark requires the recitation of Hebrew prayers and a certain degree of ceremony. Ultimately, however, Dietrich accepts that it is best to know precisely what the Ark contains before delivering it to the Führer. He allows the Ark to be carried to the ruins of an ancient Phoenician shrine—provided that armed soldiers and Nazi banners be included in the procession. The whole event will also be committed to film.

First-century replica of the ram's-head staff Moses is believed to have carried during the Jewish Exodus from Egypt

SANDS OF TIME

Expecting to find fragments of the original Ten Commandments tablets, Belloq and Dietrich are at a loss to find that the opened Ark appears to contain nothing more than sand. Gestapo agent Arnold Toht, who has privately ridiculed the quest from the start, delights in sniggering at Belloq's utter disenchantment.

Belloq's ceremonial wardrobe includes a priestly turban and headband, a checkered silk tunic, and a bejeweled pectoral, discovered among a stash of ritual objects in a treasure coffer near Jerusalem.

GRAIL CRUSADE

BRUISED AND WATERLOGGED from his misadventure in the Atlantic Ocean, Indy no sooner returns to Barnett College with the Cross of Coronado than word of his father's [dis]e sends him right back to Lisbon, Portugal, and on to Venice. [F]or the Grail makes clear, danger is equally at home in Europe [as] [un]charted regions of the globe, particularly when Fascists and Nazis [crop] up in the most unexpected places. The search for Henry begins [in] luxury but ends on horseback, with time between spent at the [helm of a] speedboat, a motorcycle, a tandem-compartment plane, and [la]cking a spare tire. But that's just Indy on the road.

From the penthouses of the lofty towers that wall Fifth Avenue, it is clear to see that Mayor Fiorello LaGuardia and Robert Moses have put their New Deal funds to good use. Manhattan's buildings have been scrubbed clean while ocean liners nuzzle at Hudson River piers and double-decker buses ferry people to all parts of what many are beginning to refer to as "the Big Apple."

[TRANSATLA]NTIC FLIGHTS

[Next year] (1939), Pan Am and others will be whisking [to Eu]rope on non-stop transatlantic flights, but [for no]w to make refueling stops along the way. [The c]onvenience when the aeroplane is a custom-[built,] just what the doctor ordered for a nervous [docto]r and a preoccupied professor on leave. [With E]arhart still missing, aviation is receiving [atten]tion, and this plane sets a new standard.

BARNETT COLLEGE, N.Y.

ST. JOHN'S, NEWFOUNDLAND

2

3

NEW YORK CITY USA

ATLANTIC OCEAN

GERMAN MILITARY MOTORBIKES

Banned by the Treaty of Versailles from engaging in aeroplane engine production, BMW turned its attention to motorcycles and created a wonder. Just last year (1937), Ernst Henne became the fastest man on two wheels by pushing a BMW to 173 mph (279.5 kph). The German military was so impressed it ordered 15,000 of the 340-cc models. With its pressed-steel star frame, rear suspension, and big saddle seat, the bike is a veritable battering ram.

PORTUGUESE COAST

The chronicles of early Spanish explorers bulge with accounts of the treacherous waters that lie between the Portuguese coast and Madeira. Hurricane season is worst but surface currents brought to boiling point by undersea volcanoes mean any time of year can be bad. Still, some crossings are worth the risk. And, with luck, a marooned traveler will meet a friendly ship navigating the turbulent sea lanes.

[...] rescues shipwrecked [Indiana Jon]es from Lisbon to New York
[The C]ross of Coronado travel [to Bar]nett College, upstate N.Y.
[The]y fly from N.Y. to St. John's, [Canad]a, Lisbon, and Venice
[Findi]ng the Knight's Tomb, [they] travel by car to Salzburg
[To free H]enry from Castle [Brunwald, they] go to Berlin by motorcycle
[With the] Grail diary, Indy and [Henry ride a] zeppelin for Athens
[They] escape the airship in a [bi]plane, but crash in Turkey
[...]s by foot, truck, and bus to [Haran, the]n by car with Sallah to Hatay
[Indy, Bro]dy, and Sallah reach the [Canyon of the] Crescent Moon on horses

---

SPECTRAL SURVEILLANCE

The explosion of a filmmaking light and a shower of sparks from the power generator signal a change. Portentous clouds gather overhead and a mist from the Ark begins to suffuse the amphitheater. Wisps of mist blend into apparitions that circle in the air and pass through the soldiers's bodies.

EYE OF THE BEHOLDER

Before Belloq's eyes, the radiantly beautiful face of one of the apparitions transforms into a ghoulish head, and Belloq becomes a channel for the Ark's destructive power. From his eyes blast bolts of raw energy, which strike and kill the awestruck soldiers.

Incinerated by an outpouring of searing heat, what remains of the soldiers and their equipment is sucked into a cyclone of energy that pierces the clouds as it climbs toward the heavens. In the end only the lid of the Ark is returned to earth.

THE TRUE ARK

Tied back-to-back to a pole, Indy warns Marion to shut her eyes. Marion's eyes are drawn toward the glow emitting from the Ark but Indiana convinces her not to look. Marion's father, Abner, had warned Indy of the Ark's power.

DON'T LOOK AT IT, MARION!

OH INDY, I MUST! IT'S BEAUTIFUL!

DO AS I SAY, MARION!

Belloq binds Indy and Marion so they will not be able to see the contents of the Ark.

FIERY DEPTHS

The Ark reserves the cruelest fates for those most directly involved in its desecration. Belloq himself becomes a column of vengeful fire, exploding in his final moments, while Dietrich and Toht, screaming in agony, melt and liquefy into oblivion.

RE-INTERRED

Indy is assured that America's top men have been assigned to investigate the Ark. In fact, it has been crated as "Army Intel # 9906753," labeled "Top Secret" and "Do Not Open," and buried among thousands of similar crates in an immense Nevada military warehouse known as Hangar 51.

THE LAST CRUSADE (1938)

T HE YEAR IS 1938, and the world is poised on the brink of a second great war. Europe and Asia are in the grip of evil forces that threaten to lay siege to the entire globe. Into this imminent wasteland strides Indiana Jones, more roving knight than archaeologist, as he embarks initially on a search for his missing father. Soon, however, Indy becomes embroiled in Henry Jones Sr.'s lifelong quest for the Holy Grail—the chalice used by Christ at the Last Supper, and believed to be capable of conferring immortality on anyone who drinks from it. The most personal of Indy's profuse adventures, the pursuit for the Grail culminates in a revelatory encounter that is both physically and emotionally healing for father and son, and replenishing for a relationship long plagued by wariness and misunderstanding.

THE ALPS

The best route from Salzburg to Berlin goes through Munich. Leaving the city's baroque architecture behind, the road passes close to Untersberg mountain, which is almost 6,000 feet (1,828.8 m) high. Legends say that the alpine mount is the resting place of Emperor Barbarossa, who will one day awake to restore the German empire to its former glory. Now that Austria is part of the Third Reich, the wait for Barbarossa has been eclipsed.

ZEPPELINS

Simply because the *Hindenburg* crashed and burned in Lakehurst, New Jersey, a year ago, it doesn't mean that travelers have anything to fear. The airship had simply sprung a gas leak; ask any of the elite passengers who still prefer zeppelin flights to aeroplanes. The *Hindenburg*'s sister ship, the *Graf Zeppelin II*, is equipped with a mail carrier plane that hangs from a sky hook under the belly—a design borrowed from the USS *Akron* and USS *Macon* airships.

ATLANTIC OCEAN

BERLIN, GERMANY ❻

CASTLE BRUNWALD SALZBURG, AUSTRIA ❺

❶ ATLANTIC COAST, PORTUGAL

❹

VENICE, ITALY

NORTHERN GREECE

SÃO MIGUEL, AZORES

LISBON, PORTUGAL

MEDITERRANEAN SEA

❼

❽

ISKENDERUN, TURKEY

❾

CANYON OF THE CRESCENT MOON

VENICE

Gondoliers on the Grand Canal wait for customers. Mussolini has stolen the Axum Obelisk from Ethiopia and had it brought to Rome; he has canceled the civil rights of Jewish Italians; and his fascist spies lurk in the shadows. Harry Pickering's bar is deserted—even Ernest Hemingway is elsewhere—and pigeons far outnumber tourists in the Piazza San Marco.

ISKENDERUN

Compared to Venice, this city could be in the tropics. The humid air is thick with citrus smells wafted in from the Nur Mountains on the yarik kaya—a hot wind that sweeps across the Mediterranean from North Africa. Restaurants cater to French troops from Syria, while Arab rug merchants have learned enough French to lure customers in for tea.

REPUBLIC OF HATAY

Names change overnight. What was Alexandretta is now Iskenderun, and what was the Autonomous Sanjak of Alexandretta is the Republic of Hatay, spreading from the Mediterranean into Turkey. South of the Nur Mountains, there are said to be churches carved from rock and a crescent-shaped canyon with an oasis once prized by ancient traders.

FORTUNE AND GLORY

Not long after the US government takes custody of the Ark of the Covenant, Indy travels to New Delhi to procure a golden statue of Shiva from a woman who needs to pay off gambling debts incurred by her husband, Rajid. Just as the deal is being concluded, Rajid bursts into the room, accusing Indy of being his wife's secret lover and shooting at him. Escaping with his life—and the statue—Jones decides that dealing with honest people is riskier than dealing with thieves. He's about to learn, however, that this isn't always the case.

Using a brass platter to shield himself from Rajid's fire, Indy breaks for the terrace. He leaps over the railing, landing on a snake charmer, whose king cobra spits venom at him.

FACULTY FRICTION

Now Professor of Archaeology at Barnett College, Indy, who has definite ideas as to how his subjects should be taught, is angered to learn that his Inca Origins seminar has been given to Professor Francisca Uribe del Arco. Francisca tries to smooth things over by inviting Jones to her home—but as soon as Indy arrives two goons try to steal a package Francisca has received from her brother Felipe, which contains a golden finger sheath from the Chimu Taya Arms of Cuzco.

THE GLORY OF THE INCA

Francisca informs Indiana that the mummies of Incan royalty were encased in golden armor and paraded on feast days. The golden forearms of the Pachacuti mummy are believed to have taken on the emperor's power to shape the monolithic stones that characterize Incan architecture.

A band of Soldiers of the Sun fall on the pair, demanding the map Indy had copied.

Francisca and Indy travel to Buenos Aires, where the search for the origin of the finger becomes a search for Felipe himself. A map concealed in an ancient text yields clues to the location of a lost city, near Lake Titicaca, in Peru.

MISSING THE BOAT

Continuing the search for the golden arms, Francisca and Indy use the services of a former Great War flying ace. Indy would like to forget his war experiences, but Antoine d'Espere thinks of little else. When a snowstorm cripples the plane, Indy and Francisca parachute to safety but d'Espere perishes. On the ground, the pair is captured by more Incan warriors, who lead them to a restored city called Tahuantinsuyu.

UP TO HIS NECK IN TROUBLE

The ruler of Tahuantinsuyu is actually Felipe, who wants to wrest control of Peru from the hands of foreign interests by using the Chimu Taya Arms to unite the people in revolt. Felipe reveals that the finger sheath was a fraud, meant to draw Indy to Peru, and that his sister was in on the scam. Their goal is to avenge their father, from whom Indy had allegedly stolen credit for an archaeological find. Taken to a mountain, Indy is dosed with coca and buried in the snow.

SPIRIT ADVISOR

Indy forces himself to overcome the anaesthetic effects of the coca and makes his way down the mountain. Searching for shelter in the cold, he finds the ruins of a way station. A shivering Jones is visited by the spirit of an aged Peruvian that leads him to a llama, whose warmth sustains Indy through a brutal night.

SUBTERRANEAN SPLENDOR

In the morning, an old man who resembles the spirit leads Indy to an island in Lake Titicaca. Ever resourceful, Indy uses gold coins stashed in his jacket to cut a deal with the islanders to guide him to the lost city indicated on the map. Jones enters an inner sanctum, where a dozen gold-encased Incan mummies are enthroned.

Among the throne room's treasures, Indy discovers the golden forearm sheaths of Emperor Pachacuti.

Agents of Transatlantic Global Mining—who had disguised themselves as the Soldiers of the Sun—are determined to keep the golden arms away from xenophobic indigenous groups.

BRINGING DOWN THE HOUSE

Donning the forearms of Pachacuti, Felipe tries to summon ancient powers, but succeeds instead in triggering an earthquake. Only Indy and Francisca survive to witness the waters of Lake Titicaca flood and hide the city forever.

THE CROSS OF CORONADO

In 1938, on a freighter carrying explosives, Indiana ends a 26-year-long quest by catching up with the man in the panama hat who made off with the Cross of Coronado when Indy was a Boy Scout. Maybe the panama man is right about Indy belonging in a museum, but so does the cross, and Indy will hurl himself into the sea rather than allow his adversary to keep it. When a wave collapses a smokestack onto the explosives, the freighter blows up, leaving on the bounding waves only Indiana, a flotation ring, and a scorched hat.

WALTER DONOVAN

Donovan sends his goons to collect Indy at Barnett College and bring him to New York City.

WALTER DONOVAN IS NOT AN ART HISTORIAN, but a passionate collector whose generous contributions to the National Museum have earned him the respect of curators and archaeologists alike. His art deco penthouse apartment on Fifth Avenue in New York City is filled with priceless pieces of art, and is frequently the site of lavish soirees hosted by his wife, who adores gold and expensive champagne. However, Walter Donovan is also a ruthless coveter of the Holy Grail, and now needs the help of Indiana Jones to obtain it.

A PIECE OF THE PAST

Indy's fluency in languages owes much to childhood disciplines imposed on him by his father.

As a test, Donovan asks Indy to translate the mid-12th-Century Latin text that appears on a sandstone monument. Unearthed by Donovan's engineers, who were mining for copper in a mountainous region north of Ankara, Turkey, the text reveals in vague terms the location of the Canyon of the Crescent Moon and the Grail sanctuary. It also states that whoever drinks from the Grail will have "a spring inside him, welling up for eternal life." Jones, however, dismisses all of it as a bedtime story, and initially rejects Donovan's offer to search for the Grail—until he learns that Donovan's missing project leader is none other than his father.

Donovan believes that the fragment is one of two markers left behind by three knights of the First Crusade, who found the Grail 1,000 years after it disappeared from its original sanctuary in England. Indy also discovers a rubbing of the fragment in his father's treasured Grail diary.

FRIENDS IN BAD PLACES

Henry Jones Sr. knows that Donovan is ruled by his passions—and that he would probably sell his mother for an Etruscan vase. But even Henry is surprised to learn of Donovan's Nazi affiliations. In fact, Donovan considers himself to be above petty politics and ordinary morality. With the power of the Grail, he trusts he'll soon be above mortality, as well, drinking to his own health when Hitler has "gone the way of the dodo."

COLONEL VOGEL

A Nazi through and through, Vogel cares more about carrying out his orders than he does about Henry's Grail diary or the fabled cup itself. Hitler's go-between with Dr. Schneider, he is eager to kill Indy and Henry after the diary has been obtained, if only to avenge the deaths of the Nazi soldiers mowed down by Indy shortly after they had burst into Henry's room. Later, still infuriated by the indignity of having been hurled from a zeppelin, Vogel takes sadistic delight in punishing Jones during the attack on a convoy in Hatay, garroting him with a chain, forcing his face against a tank tread, stomping on his hands when he is clutching onto a shredded gun barrel, and hammering him with a shovel. Fitting, then, that this maniacal man should plummet to his death aboard an out-of-control war machine.

Elsa and Vogel make a good team when they trick Indy into surrendering the Grail diary. Only Henry knows that Vogel wouldn't kill a confederate—except in the line of duty.

"Didn't I warn you not to trust anybody, Dr. Jones?"
—Walter Donovan

CAN'T TAKE IT WITH YOU

Donovan laments Indy's lack of vision regarding his allegiance to the Nazi cause, confessing that he is interested in the Grail itself, not in writing himself into history. When Indiana refuses to complete the quest, Donovan heartlessly forces Indy to undertake the challenges of the Grail temple by shooting his father, who suddenly needs the healing power of the cup to survive.

Walter Donovan had to wonder why everybody assumed him to be on the American side simply because he resided there.

HIS CUP RUNNETH OVER

Donovan has been warned: by the Brotherhood of the Cruciform Sword, protectors of the Grail, who said that the cup of life holds eternal damnation for the unrighteous; by Marcus Brody, who counseled that he was meddling with powers he couldn't possibly comprehend; and by the Grail Knight, who stated that the false grail would take life rather than extend it. He fails even to heed his own advice about placing trust in others, when he follows Dr. Schneider's orders and drinks from the cup she chooses.

THE FRIAR'S TALE

Among Donovan's collection of antiquities is an ancient leather-bound manuscript with hand-painted pages. It tells the story, related to a Franciscan friar, of the three knights who found the Grail, and of the two markers they left behind. Indy is shocked to find that what he believed to be a tall story is, in fact, true.

Hints in the manuscript led Henry to a library in Venice.

ELSA SCHNEIDER

A SILVER MEDAL WINNER in the 50-meter freestyle at the 1932 Olympic Games, Austrian art historian Dr. Elsa Schneider is everything Indy could want in a partner, save for one thing: she is also a Nazi agent. But even that is a deception. While she gives all appearances of being loyal to the Third Reich, she weeps in secret at Hitler's book burning rally in Berlin and values the Holy Grail far more than she does the swastika. Indeed, Schneider is so obsessed with acquiring Henry Jones Sr.'s Grail diary that she willingly takes both him and Indiana as lovers.

When Indy produces a partial rubbing of Donovan's tablet, Elsa recognizes it as the one Henry had, and is certain that Indy is in possession of the diary.

The decomposed skull of the long-buried crusader bobs to the surface of the foul water.

OIL AND WATER

Neither Elsa nor Indy is aware that adversaries have followed them into the depths of the library in Venice. It isn't long before a fire begins to spread through the catacombs. Taking refuge under the crusader's overturned sarcophagus, Elsa is forced to fend off scores of panicked rats that clutch at her hair. She loathes having to rely on a man for assistance, but breathes a sigh of relief when Indy finds a way out.

QUICK LEARNER

Elsa grabs the steering wheel of a speedboat while Indy fights off an agent of the Brotherhood of the Cruciform Sword, ignorant of the fact that he is battling with a potential ally in the search for Henry Jones. Skillfully maneuvering the speedboat, Elsa leads their pursuers on a wild ride.

After Elsa shows Indy the Austrian way of saying good-bye, Colonel Vogel uses his balled fist to demonstrate the German way.

"I believe in the Grail, not the swastika."
—Elsa Schneider

A SIMPLE MISUNDERSTANDING

Elsa—who Henry Sr. claims says "Mein Führer" when she talks in her sleep—apologizes to Indy for having been deceptive from the start. She is certain, though, that Indy would have done the same, if it had meant coming even one step closer to the Grail. When she tells Indy that she will never forget their wonderful time together, Henry thinks she is referring to *their* wonderful time, and thanks her.

UP IN FLAMES

At a book-burning rally at the Institute of Aryan Culture in Berlin, Indy retrieves Henry's Grail diary from Elsa. She has kept it for herself rather than turn it over to the Reich Museum, as ordered by Colonel Vogel. The fact that Elsa denies being a brownshirt and has prevented the diary from being incinerated isn't nearly enough to persuade Indiana that she is one of the good guys. Indy has learnt his lesson about trusting people.

Elsa refuses to accept that the search for the Grail requires purity of heart.

Chalice liberated from Constantinople by the Knights Templar

ETERNAL LIFE

In the Grail sanctuary, Elsa insists on being the one to distinguish the Grail cup from a vast assortment of similar cups. She reveals the depths of her cunning when she selects the shiniest, most jewel-encrusted of the bunch. Offering it to Donovan as the real item, she gives Indy a look that suggests she is doing it for Indy and Henry's sake.

AT HER FINGERTIPS

Indy is willing to forgive Elsa for all she has done, but greed dooms her. Grabbing the Grail after Indy has had his father drink from it, she flees across the Great Seal embossed on the floor of the temple atrium, heedless of the Grail Knight's warning not to cross this boundary. Pitched along with the Grail into a crevasse opened by tectonic forces, she still has a chance to choose love over death, but chooses poorly.

Indy is so blinded by Elsa's beauty he fails to realize that he is being deceived.

Niches contain bodies of Franciscan monks and eighth Century Christian clergy

The absence of oxygen means that the wooden piles remain intact, even after centuries under water

Old well still collects rainwater run-off from piazza

Hidden prayer room

Medieval members of the Brotherhood of the Cruciform Sword buried here

Sarcophagus of St. Mark the Evangelist

Canal joins Grand Canal near Rialto Bridge

Brotherhood ignite petrol to stop Indy and Elsa finding the Knights tomb

Forgotten annex of catacombs

Stained glass window containing vital clues

Columns plundered from Constantinople after Fourth Crusade

Mosaic tiled floor conceals entrance to extensive network of hidden catacombs

Monks used skulls and bones to create designs on walls

Tombs have been constructed at a lower level than surrounding canals

Swarm of rats flee blazing river

45 million-year-old fossil

Tunnels flood as Venice continues to sink

Knight's tomb in ancient chapel of rest

Indy and Elsa turn coffin upside down in the water to escape the flames

Thousands of wooden piles form foundations for buildings, bridges, and pavements

Tomb network connects to original sewer system

Members of the Brotherhood have knocked out Marcus Brody and dragged him behind the bookcases

Workers unload barrels of newly arrived virgin olive oil

❶ STANDING BENEATH a stained-glass window that had been re-created in Henry's Grail diary, Indy, Marcus Brody, and Elsa Schneider attempt to decipher the meaning of the Roman numbers Henry jotted on a scrap of paper.

❷ BY THE LIGHT of an improvised torch, Indy and Elsa—having broken through a marble floor tile— wend their way through the rat-infested and partially flooded catacombs in search of Sir Richard's sarcophagus.

VENICE

MOST OF THE STRUCTURES built on Venice's original archipelago of 118 islands are supported on closely spaced wooden piles, driven deep into the soft clay and sand bed of the shallow lagoon. But the early Christian monks, whose monastery predates the church that now adorns the Piazza San Marco as a library, labored in secret for centuries to create a warren of stone-walled water-tight passageways beneath the building. Sir Richard, who, with his two brothers found the Holy Grail, traveled to the Republic of Venice. By the time he reached the city, the tunnels had become catacombs and the knight himself was ultimately interred there.

Church once housed impoverished members of aristocracy in state-provided apartments

Imposing Classical facade of Renaissance church that is now a library

Pigeons are descended from original group released from Basilica on Palm Sunday, 1200 CE

Square is paved with Istrian marble

Piazza San Marco is the center of Venice

3 WHEN MEMBERS of the Brotherhood of the Cruciform Sword—protectors of the Holy Grail—set the catacombs ablaze, Indy and Elsa swim for safety through a sewer line, emerging amid tourists lunching alfresco in the piazza.

4 KAZIM AND OTHER Brotherhood members traveled to Venice from Iskenderun when they were notified of Henry's nosing about in the library. They now pursue Indy and Elsa across the Venice lagoon in wooden speedboats.

Crates contain leather goods, hand-blown glassware, and other exports

Blackshirt operatives exchange intelligence data

Seafood risotto is a house specialty and popular with tourists

Railway serves industrial area

3

Indy and Elsa will emerge from sewer drain into the square

Ladder to the surface

Indy and Elsa will flee along this sewer

Old harbor area and boat repair yard

Traditional Venetian mooring posts

Left side of the gondola is made longer than the right to counterbalance weight of gondolier

Harbor Master's office

The Venice lagoon leads to dockyards and open-sea

4

Harbor Master does his own laundry

Speedboats for hire, tied up at harbor side

Fishing boat used in movie shown at first Venice Film Festival

Coal in barge conceals contraband rifles imported from Greece

THE GRAIL DIARY

AN UNASSUMING CALF LEATHER-BOUND JOURNAL, banded with an elastic tie, Henry Jones Sr.'s diary contains sketches and jottings about the Holy Grail dating back to his student days at Oxford and his tenure as Professor of Medieval Literature at Princeton University. A silver dollar certificate and train tickets serve as bookmarks, and miscellaneous sheets of notes and sculpture rubbings are interspersed among the journal's 282 pages. During the Nazi pursuit for ancient objects of power, Henry's diary, for a time, becomes as sought after as the Grail itself.

A LABOR OF LOVE

A fixation long before the death of his wife, Henry's Grail studies became an obsession afterward. In his homes in Utah and New Jersey, Henry spent long hours poring over rare books and aged manuscripts, meticulously copying illustrations. Dragged through Asia Minor and the Far East on quests for clues, young Indy realized that, in his father's eyes, he would always take second place to the Grail; he suspects that his mother had felt the same.

A quote from George Washington tells Henry that no joy be derived from an enemy's misfortune.

A FINE MESS

Henry's Princeton office is filled with out-of-print volumes and reproductions of artwork related to the Grail legend. When Walter Donovan learns that Henry's Grail diary has gone missing, Donovan has Henry's Princeton office and his home turned upside down. Henry was rightly suspicious when he was hired by Donovan to lead the search for the Grail and he sent the diary to Indy at Barnett College. Shortly afterward, he was abducted in Venice by Nazi agents.

Los Angeles Railyard train ticket

Stained-glass design is reminiscent of an 18th-Century tarot card from the suit of swords.

THE LOW ROAD

As meticulous as he was, Henry frequently entered his jottings while in motion—aboard trains, boats, or horse-drawn carriages—and often in the middle of the night. Some of the maps were based on nothing more than conversations with scholars, holy men, or local guides.

DEAR DIARY

Pressed into a crowd of autograph seekers in front of the Institute of Aryan Culture in Berlin, Indy finds himself face to face with Adolf Hitler. He mistakes Indy for just another fanatic and scrawls his signature on a page of the Grail diary.

A sketch of the window in the Venice library appears in the Grail diary, juxtaposed with references to Melchizedek, a Biblical king. A drawing of a chalice is obviously not the Grail itself, but one found by Henry at some point during his extensive travels.

The stag drinking from the chalice is a symbol of the soul's thirst for God. The facing drawing is of the upper portion of the window in the Venice library, which Henry dates as 14th Century.

A CRUCIAL CLUE

A Flemish painting of the crucifixion hangs in Henry's parlor, showing Joseph of Arimathea capturing Christ's spilled blood in a chalice. Henry viewed the original artwork in July 1906, during a visit to a French castle that contained Grail artifacts. He believed the painter was a friar who received an account of the Grail from a knight of the First Crusade.

Map of the southern region of Judeah was based on on-site interviews with shepherds and traders.

Entries related to the story of the biblical Lycurgus stress the importance of sacrifice in those seeking the Grail.

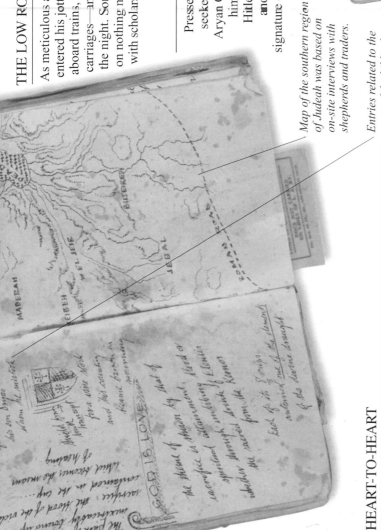

HEART-TO-HEART

On the zeppelin, Indy wants to talk about the past. Henry, however, will discuss only the distant past: specifically, the three challenges that face those who enter the Grail temple, translated from Latin as the Breath of God, the Word of God, and the Path of God. Henry bookmarks this diary page with a second Los Angeles Railyard train ticket.

CASTLE BRUNWALD

ON THE HUNT FOR HENRY, Indy and Elsa drive to Castle Brunwald, which all but straddles the German-Austrian border. A rambling manse of turrets and ramparts lorded over by snarling gargoyles, the castle's sinister aspects are accentuated by flashes of lightning that accompany the duo's arrival. Elsa claims to know only that the Salzburg Brunwalds are art collectors, but, in fact, she is leading Indy into a maze of betrayals that will make him question everything he accepts as fact.

Borrowing Elsa's beret and cape-like coat, Indy barges in to Castle Brunwald, claiming to be a Scottish lord keen on seeing the castle tapestries.

KID'S PLAY

It isn't long before Jones discovers that the castle is concealing a nest of Nazis—and Indy *hates* those guys, as he tells Elsa. He locates where his father is being held captive simply by finding the room that has been wired with an alarm. Instantly, Indy uncoils his whip, and swings from a ledge in an adjoining room to a gargoyle, then through the windows of his father's room. His rescue attempt is almost shortlived when he is smashed over the head by Henry himself, wielding a Ming vase.

Relieved to learn that the vase is a fake, Henry listens in rapt attention to Indy's account of the discovery of Sir Richard's tomb in Venice's rat-infested catacombs. But the happy reunion is cut short by three Nazis who burst into the room demanding the Grail diary.

"I told you—don't call me Junior!"

—*Indiana Jones*

GOOD OLE DAD

At first Henry can't accept that Indy would be foolish enough to bring the diary with him on a rescue mission. The fact that Indy has prompts Henry to exclaim that he would have been better off mailing it to the Marx Brothers! The escalating argument and Henry's needling use of the diminutive "Junior" finally tips Indy over the edge. Snatching a machinegun from one of the soldiers, he kills all three with a spray of fire, leaving Henry aghast at what his son has done.

Henry knows that Colonel Vogel's threat to kill Elsa is empty. Unlike his naïve son, Henry never trusted Elsa or Donovan, but played along regardless, in the hope of coming one step closer to finding the Holy Grail.

FOOL ME ONCE

Elsa reveals her true nature when she slips the diary from the pocket of Indy's leather jacket, apologizing not for having put him in a position where he is forced to surrender the diary but for deceiving him to begin with. Backing away to join Colonel Vogel, a look of cold-blooded triumph surfaces on her face. Later, Elsa's plans to hunt for Brody, who holds some missing Grail diary pages, are quashed when Vogel tells her that she is needed in Berlin for a book-burning rally at the Institute of Aryan Culture.

Jones looks on smugly, as Walter Donovan and Elsa realize that Indy has torn the map from the Grail diary. Without the map, the diary is no more than a curio.

FROM THE FIRE TO THE FÜHRER

Tied back to back, Indy and Henry make a discovery in the hearth of the blazing room. Indy's knee taps an andiron and the rear panel of the fireplace revolves, opening on a Nazi command center. Here, the Nazis are monitoring the activities of their agents and saboteurs in Czechoslovakia and Poland, in preparation for blitzes into both countries—intelligence Indy will later pass along to England's secret service, MI6.

So much for my shamrock cigarette lighter being a lucky charm, Indy thought.

Having fled the castle, Indy dispatches several Nazi motorcyclists—playing the knight he will eventually become when he arrives at the Grail sanctuary. It isn't enough to impress or amuse his father. Henry would much rather wind his pocket watch than afford his son an ounce of recognition.

CROSS-PURPOSES

Indy and Henry's conflict grows personal at the crossroads, when Indy receives a slap across the face for using Christ's name in a blasphemous manner. Henry insists that they go to Berlin to recover the Grail diary rather than to Iskenderun to rescue Marcus Brody and the map. For the quest for the Grail is not an archaeological one but a race against evil, where there's no medal for finishing in second place. And only with the diary in hand will Henry and Indy be successful in navigating the Grail sanctuary's cunningly lethal booby traps.

ESCAPE FROM BERLIN

PILGRIMS IN AN UNHOLY LAND, Indy and Henry arrive in Berlin, where Indy quickly procures a uniform from a knocked-out Nazi soldier and searches for Elsa Schneider among a throng of brownshirts and civilians. Spying Elsa, Jones roughly relieves her of Henry's Grail diary, and has to restrain himself from doing her greater damage. Despite her assertion that she is not a loyal Nazi, she blows the whistle on Indy soon after he has reclaimed the book. Indy and Henry's journey from Berlin will not be an easy passage.

Books of all sorts fuel a huge bonfire in front of the Institute of Aryan Culture, while Adolf Hitler addresses the crowd. Indy doesn't want the Grail diary to join the pile of volumes.

FIRST CLASS ONLY

Colonel Vogel and several plainclothes Gestapo agents are already on the lookout for Indy and Henry when they arrive at Berlin's aerodrome. Booking passage on a zeppelin bound for Athens, the pair no sooner find seats than Vogel boards the airship and identifies Henry. Indy, however, takes matters into his own hands, allowing father and son to engage in a brief heart-to-heart conversation. Indy is eager to discuss the gulf that has separated them for twenty years. But Henry, true to form, is interested mostly in addressing the trio of challenges they will face when they reach the Grail temple.

The LZ-138 zeppelin is modeled after the Hindenburg, which crossed the Atlantic in a record-breaking forty-two hours.

Donning yet another appropriated uniform, Indy deals with Vogel by pretending to be a ship's steward, and literally throwing the colonel off the airship when he fails to produce a ticket.

BELLY OF THE BEAST

Indy and Henry's peaceful interlude is interrupted when the zeppelin starts to return to Berlin. Gaining access to the airship's interior, Indy—back in fedora and leather jacket, and toting his father's valise and umbrella—hurries Henry along a catwalk that accesses a modified Buecher biplane affixed to the airship's undercarriage.

IT TAKES TWO TO DOGFIGHT

Clambering down into the biplane, Indy and Henry prepare to make their escape. Henry is surprised to learn that Indy knows how to fly—but disconcerted to hear that he doesn't know how to land. Releasing the plane from the zeppelin, Indy spots two German fighter-bombers zooming in to nip at their tail.

Indy watched the Messerschmitt complete its tight arc and leap at them with guns blazing.

"Sharing your adventures is an interesting experience."

—Henry Jones

ELEVEN-O'CLOCK HIGH

Giving Henry a quick lesson in aerial combat terminology, Indy instructs him to man the tail gun. Henry fixes the gun's sights on one of the Luftwaffe fighter-bombers and opens fire, traversing the weapon and making mincemeat of the biplane's rear stabilizer. With maneuverability lost, Indy assumes that they've taken a hit, which Henry disingenuously affirms.

Scampering out of the crash-landed craft, Indy and Henry waste no time stealing a car from a man who is in the middle of changing a tire. Nothing will stand in the way of their escape.

LOW CLEARANCE

The Stuka pilot pursues the car into a tunnel. Its wings sheared from the fuselage, the plane bellies through the tunnel and explodes. With one fighter still in the sky, Indy and Henry find themselves on an isolated beach with nowhere to hide. Henry, however, manages to scare a flock of seagulls into panicked flight, some of which rise into the fighter's path, causing it to crash into a hillside.

Henry credits Emperor Charlemagne for his brave action, citing the passage for Indy: "Let my armies be the rocks and the trees and the birds in the sky."

MY KINGDOM FOR A CAR

With Marcus Brody in captivity and Henry's map to the Grail sanctuary now in hand, Walter Donovan and Vogel cut a deal with the Sultan of Hatay for safe passage through his lands. Initially, Donovan offers the Sultan artworks and golden items the Nazis have acquired from some of the finest families in Germany, but the Sultan prefers Donovan's Rolls Royce Phantom Two.

THE GRAIL TEMPLE

HENRY'S GRAIL DIARY contains a map without names, showing an oasis, a south-flowing river, and a narrow gorge. The text on the tablet fragment uncovered by Donovan's survey team in Turkey names the gorge as the Canyon of the Crescent Moon, and verifies that it is located "across the desert and through the mountains," but provides no starting point—until Indy discovers the sarcophagus of Sir Richard in Venice, and the engraved shield that names Alexandretta. Destroyed after a year-long siege by Crusaders, Alexandretta was rebuilt as the modern city of Iskenderun, in the Republic of Hatay. With all this information, locating the Grail temple is finally within reach.

Ancient inscriptions told of an entrance "broad enough for only one man." But Walter Donovan lacks the patience of a true seeker, and so dynamites a gap into the wall that shelters the temple, and leads Elsa Schneider and the remaining soldiers into the canyon.

A GRECO-ROMAN WONDER

Carved into a sheer, rose-colored wall of sandstone in a narrow gorge prone to flash floods is the columned façade of the Grail temple itself, "holy enough for all men, where the cup that holds the blood of Jesus Christ resides." Indy, Henry, Sallah, and Marcus ride onto the scene an hour or so after Donovan's party has entered the temple. The group make their way inside the temple just in time to witness the beheading of the second Turkish soldier whom Donovan has forced to face the temple's first challenge.

Moments after entering the temple, Indy, Henry, Sallah, and Marcus are discovered and held at gunpoint.

THE WASTELAND

Shot point blank in the abdomen by Donovan, Henry collapses to the floor, his former expression of rapture yielding to one of agony. Donovan's only motive is to force Indy to go down in history as the one to return with the Grail. The wasteland Indy has been thrust into requires that he come to terms with what he believes and accept that the search for the Grail is the search for the divine in oneself.

THE THREE CHALLENGES

Only the penitent man can pass the challenge known as the Breath of God. Indy understands at the last second that this means God is to be approached humbly, on one's knees. Narrowly avoiding a beheading, Indy proceeds to the next test, where he must walk in the Word of God or name of God, written as it was in Latin when the temple was built. Indy then reaches the final test—the Path of God. He is required to make a leap of faith into a crevasse of immeasurable depth, which is in fact spanned by a forced-perspective stone bridge.

KNIGHT OF THE REALM

In many ways, Indy is his father's proxy. He crawls through a tunnel that opens on the Grail Sanctuary, where he finds an aged knight reading the Bible by firelight. This crusader is the bravest and most worthy of the three brothers who had sworn to protect the Grail 700 years earlier. As Indy enters the sanctuary, the knight raises a two-handed broadsword in combat, only to be toppled by the weight of the weapon. He admits defeat and surrenders care of the Grail to the curiously dressed knight who vanquished him—Indy.

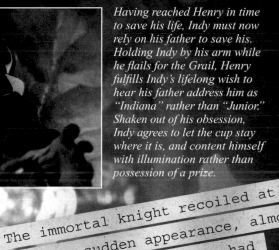

RAPID AGING

What Indy had earlier dismissed as an old man's dream becomes an old man's nightmare when Walter Donovan drinks from a bejeweled chalice. Elsa has chosen the chalice from among dozens of cups arrayed on an arc of stone altar. Realizing in his last moments of life that he has been tricked, Donovan turns on Elsa, attempting to take her into whatever hell is waiting for him.

Indy is not dazzled by the jewels and gold. Under the watchful gaze of Elsa and the Grail Knight, he chooses a blemished, unadorned, metal-lined goblet with a stout base. With his father's life at stake, he drinks from the font, deeply and wisely.

"He chose . . . poorly."
—Grail Knight

Having reached Henry in time to save his life, Indy must now rely on his father to save his. Holding Indy by his arm while he flails for the Grail, Henry fulfills Indy's lifelong wish to hear his father address him as "Indiana" rather than "Junior." Shaken out of his obsession, Indy agrees to let the cup stay where it is, and content himself with illumination rather than possession of a prize.

The immortal knight recoiled at Donovan's sudden appearance, almost as if evil incarnate had entered the chamber.

FADING LIGHT

Henry quickly gets over the fact that, after a lifetime of preparation, he didn't enter the Grail sanctuary. Had he been first into the chamber, it is conceivable that he might have remained there as guardian of the cup. But he ultimately feels enlightened by the adventure.

GRAIL TRAIL

SHAPED BY TECTONIC PLATE ACTIVITY, the Canyon of the Crescent Moon is actually made up of a series of parallel gorges, some of which are immeasurably deep. The Grail Temple is hewn from a palisade of sandstone that forms the walls of both the shallowest and deepest gorges, and is undermined by fault lines. Constructed by a secret society of Aramaic-speaking Semites that came to be called the Brotherhood of the Cruciform Sword, the temple contains a trio of cunningly lethal traps that make use of the gorges and the canyon's perpetual water source. The cave that houses the cup of Christ was a sanctuary long before the arrival of the three Crusaders who had found the Grail.

Hatay soldier guards the entrance to the temple

Statues of sentinel knights modelled on two knights that returned to Europe, leaving their brother in the Temple

Stone lions represent Christ, the Lion of the tribe of Judea

Alternating layers of porous and non-porous rock direct water flow

Greco-Roman facade was present before the Grail Temple was constructed in 1000 CE

Columns, architrave, and frieze are reinforced to withstand quakes

Horses ridden in from canyon entrance

Marcus comforts wounded Henry, while Donovan and Elsa await Indy's return

Great Seal bears sigil of the Brotherhood of the Cruciform Sword

Deep geological faults extend the length of the canyon

1 *PARTING COBWEBS* and ignoring the decapitated bodies on the floor, Indy moves into the dark passageway at the top of the stairs, asking himself how a penitent man should approach God.

2 *SURVEYING THE ARRAY* of cups, chalices, and other artifacts that crowd the Grail chamber's semicircular altar, Walter Donovan foolishly leaves the final choice about the Grail to Elsa.

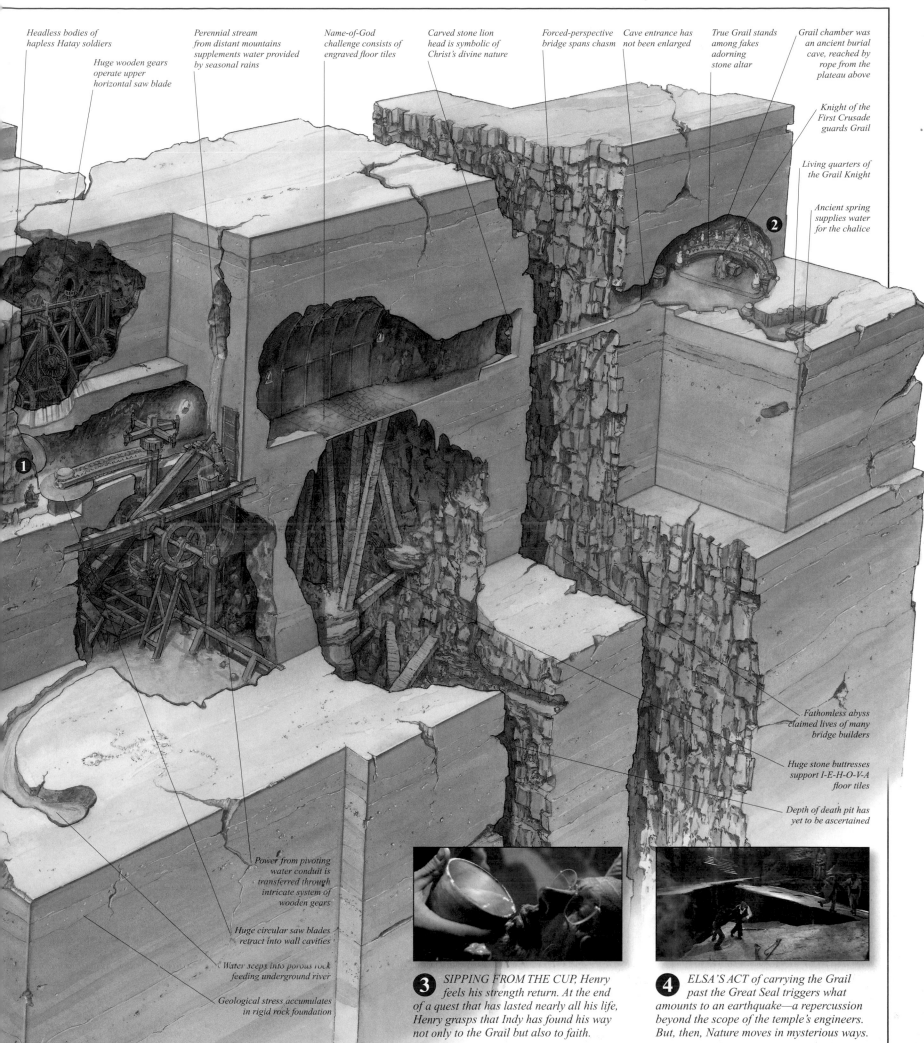

Headless bodies of
hapless Hatay soldiers

Huge wooden gears
operate upper
horizontal saw blade

Perennial stream
from distant mountains
supplements water provided
by seasonal rains

Name-of-God
challenge consists of
engraved floor tiles

Carved stone lion
head is symbolic of
Christ's divine nature

Forced-perspective
bridge spans chasm

Cave entrance has
not been enlarged

True Grail stands
among fakes
adorning
stone altar

Grail chamber was
an ancient burial
cave, reached by
rope from the
plateau above

Knight of the
First Crusade
guards Grail

Living quarters of
the Grail Knight

Ancient spring
supplies water
for the chalice

Fathomless abyss
claimed lives of many
bridge builders

Huge stone buttresses
support I-E-H-O-V-A
floor tiles

Depth of death pit has
yet to be ascertained

Power from pivoting
water conduit is
transferred through
intricate system of
wooden gears

Huge circular saw blades
retract into wall cavities

Water seeps into porous rock
feeding underground river

Geological stress accumulates
in rigid rock foundation

3 SIPPING FROM THE CUP, Henry
feels his strength return. At the end
of a quest that has lasted nearly all his life,
Henry grasps that Indy has found his way
not only to the Grail but also to faith.

4 ELSA'S ACT of carrying the Grail
past the Great Seal triggers what
amounts to an earthquake—a repercussion
beyond the scope of the temple's engineers.
But, then, Nature moves in mysterious ways.

FURTHER ADVENTURES

Henry Jones Sr. would be the first to say that his son has spent as much of his life running from things as he has running toward them. As World War II dawns, little has changed—neither Indy's outfit nor the length of his stride, nor even the company he keeps. Only the opponents have changed. More often than not they are intent on nothing less than world domination. Such adversaries know no limits, and will use even the people Indy holds dearest to claw their way to the top—and loose their maniacal evil on the world.

THUNDER IN THE ORIENT

EAGER TO ESCAPE THE CLASSROOM, Indy jumps at the chance to work as an epigrapher for a French-led archaeological team excavating the Tunisian site of Bas Shamra. At the end of Indy's stint, Barnett College's share of the site's 3,000-year-old clay slates are saved from bandits, thanks to a fast thinking young orphan named Khamal. Skilled with a knife, and with a nose for sniffing out treasure, Khamal becomes so attached to Indy that when a mysterious telegram from Marcus Brody sends Indy to Nepal, Khamal stows away on the plane that carries Indy there.

Indy is surprised to learn that his old acquaintance and archaeologist-turned-psychic, Sophia Hapgood, has requested his help.

THE COVENANT OF BUDDHA

Sophia has discovered a sheaf of palm-leaf scrolls that seem to have been dictated by Gutama Buddha and speak of a covenant detailing Buddha's enlightenment. This is verified by a blind holy man who appears on the scene to tell of a divine revelation by Buddha that remains hidden in a secret shrine—which has the power to unite the 500 million Buddhists across Asia. Overhearing as much, a rival archaeologist named van Aaken attempts to make off with the palm-leaf scrolls by taking Khamal hostage.

Van Aaken would have done better to take Sophia hostage than Khamal. A kick from the kid and a lash from Indy's whip send van Aaken packing.

Whip in one hand, revolver in the other, Indy fights as savagely as any of the warriors.

QUEST FOR THE ASIAN GRAIL

The king of Nepal agrees to lend his support to a search for the Covenant, including the services of anthropologist Dr. Patar Kali, who guides Indy, Sophia, and their team of Sherpas through the Khyber Pass into the Afghan regions. There, they are attacked by tribal warriors who capture Sophia. But when she proves too rambunctious for even their taste, the Waziri clan offer her as a prize in a ritual buz kashi race, in which a headless sand-stuffed calf substitutes for a ball. Demonstrating superior riding skills, a disguised Indy effectively wins the race, rescuing Sophia with the help of dynamite charges detonated by Patar.

THE COLOSSUS OF BAMIAN

Japanese General Masashi Kyojo's Nipponese troops reveal themselves as competitors for the Covenant when Indy, Sophia, and the rest are en route to Afghanistan's Bamian Valley, renowned for a giant statue of Buddha carved into a cliff-face. The Sherpas clamber to the summit of the statue, where Khamal's keen nose guides Indy to a hidden map. But before Indy can make sense of it all, a sumo-sized Japanese soldier nearly beheads him with a samurai sword.

A Chanri-Ha warrior-shaman attempts to ward off the new arrivals.

LOST HORIZON

In the Hindu Kush mountain range, Indy and Sophia are led to the city of Chanri-Ha that initially appears to have inspired author James Hilton's description of Shangri-La. The locals embrace Khamal as the reincarnation of their god, Zan-Khan but it is not long before the group are being attacked by warriors and are forced to flee.

SERPENT LADY

The group is joined by an allegedly mute slave girl, who turns out to be Serpent Lady, the leader of a nomadic insurgent force opposed to Chiang Kai-Shek. To Indy, though, she is yet another misguided revolutionary, poured from the same mold as Pancho Villa and it is not long before she enters the race to find the Covenant. When Kyojo tries to capture Indy and Sophia, the warrior queen's loyal forces seal the ravine that serves as a shortcut to Szechwan Province of China—and the sanctuary of the Covenant.

RAILROADED

Professor Jones has long lost hope that the slave they had named Lotus Flower will repay him and Sophia for the kindness they showed her in Chanri-Ha. And matters just keep getting worse. Waylaying a train filled with soldiers of Chiang Kai-Shek's liberation army, Serpent Lady assassinates the commanding officer for the abuses his forces heaped upon her land and people; sends the wealthy passengers fleeing for their lives from their private cars; and commandeers the train.

KYOJO KNOWS BEST

In the race for the Covenant, General Kyojo leaves behind as many Japanese bodies as Chinese, by demanding ritual suicide of those who have failed him. Kyojo views China's resistance to Japan's "peaceful" mission as yet another example of the antiquated ideologies that plague the nation, which the general and his ilk wish only to modernize, in the same way Western nations helped invigorate feudalistic Japan.

BITES THE DUST

General Kyojo has a surprise waiting for Indy, Sophia, and Serpent Lady in the city of Hankow, in the form of soldiers, artillery, and a squadron of Mitsubishi Zeros. But unknown to Kyojo, his adversaries had abandoned the train ahead of schedule and entered Szechwan by crossing the Yangtze River. There, however, Serpent Lady is captured by Ch'ao the Red, a full-bearded Chinese warlord, who ultimately falls to Khamal's knife and a round fired by Indy when Ch'ao sets his sights on Sophia.

Indy, Sophia, Khamal, and Patar are saved from being torn limb from limb by Ch'ao's enraged fighters when Japanese dive bombers drop their payloads on Szechwan. Seizing an armored vehicle, the quartet, reunited with Serpent Lady, race for the Buddhist temple complex that houses the Covenant.

FOUND AND LOST

The armored car is overturned by a Japanese bomb and the Japanese are first to arrive at the ruins. Hurrying after Kyojo, Indy and Patar take him by surprise and unearth the rolled scrolls that comprise the Covenant. Cursing himself for not knowing better, Indy watches the scrolls as they deteriorate, exposed to the air for the first time in centuries. Then a tremor sends the chest that contains them into a deep abyss, where they are lost to everyone.

SARGASSO PIRATES

COLD WATER QUICKLY BECOMES hot water when Indy hires peg-legged Captain Bill Lawton and his cutthroat crew to transport him to the icy North Atlantic in search of a relic thought to be an ancient Viking boat. Lawton has held a grudge against Indy since the sinking of the *Vazquez de Coronado* off the Portugal coast, as a consequence of Indy's single-minded pursuit of the fabled Cross of Coronado. Despite the fact that Indy saved the captain from being fully devoured by sharks at the time, Lawton tries to kill Indy at the first opportunity. His murderous attempt occurs just when they discover the Viking ship on an iceberg, along with a battle axe that belonged to explorer Leif Ericsson, which has a treasure map etched on it.

Lawson might have had his revenge if not for the intervention of a polar bear. Sparing the captain's life, Indy shoots the bear. But by then, the crew has marooned them.

CAIRO AND NEW JERSEY JONES

YOUR FLOATING CRAP GAME JUST SPRANG A LEAK, NEW JERSEY. YOU CAN'T SCAM YOUR *BLUE BLOODS* WITH THE *REAL MCCOY* IN TOWN.

HAVE *FAITH*, CAIRO. AFTER ALL, WASN'T I ABLE TO SLIP A *WANTED WOMAN* PAST THE AUTHORITIES?

Rescued by the luxury liner *Normandie* when the iceberg drifts into shipping lanes, Indy learns that one of the passengers—a con man named New Jersey Jones—has been claiming to be Indy's brother. Traveling with him is a shady lady known as Cairo, in flight from trouble of an unspecified sort. Lawton, who recognizes Cairo, cuts a deal with her to ensnare Indy, but the plan goes horribly wrong, leaving Indy, Cairo, Lawton, and New Jersey Jones adrift in a lifeboat.

NO WAY OUT

As many a derelict vessel is wont to do, the lifeboat ends up mired in the Sargasso Sea, a vast expanse of becalmed, seaweed-laden waters known also as "the graveyard of lost ships." And yet in among a flotilla of stranded galleons and man-o'-wars, Indy encounters a band of pirates who have made a home for themselves by lashing ships together and plundering those that drift in.

WELCOME, VISITORS, TO *SARGASSO BAY* -- THE CITY OF SHIPS!

THE LAWTON MUTINY

With some of the ships dating back to the fifteenth century, Indy is eager to get a look at the historical treasures they might hold, especially aboard *The Freedom*, the private ship of a female pirate known to her followers as The Sea Witch. After being made to walk the plank by The Sea Witch and almost succumbing to a kraken, Indy reboards *The Freedom*, discovering more treasure than he imagined. Meanwhile, Lawton and some of the pirates stage a mutiny, during which The Sea Witch is shot and Indy is blamed.

Judged guilty of murdering The Sea Witch, Indy is forced to undergo a pirate torture called "a sweating," which calls for the guilty party to be chained to a ship's mizzenmast and forced to circle it while being beaten, whipped, and slashed by the crew. Indy is saved from death at the last moment when a fire breaks out.

THE WOLF BOAT

With much of the ship crisped by the flames, a Grey Wolf U-boat, previously trapped by the seaweeds, rises to the surface. Among the pirates is an aged German sub captain who assures Lawton that he can pilot the U-boat. However, when he faces off with Lawton, Lawton realizes Jones would make a better first mate.

TREASURES OF THE SARGASSO

The treasure Indy finds on The Freedom fills the small cabin space in which it is hidden. The oceanic currents have steered the various treasures to the Sargasso: Greek, Minoan, and Venetian antiquities, and enough pieces-of-eight, gems, and jewels to build a museum to house the find.

GOING TO GUNS

Indy is surprised and relieved to learn that The Sea Witch is alive, thanks to Cairo tending to her wounds. But the trio needs to act quickly to keep from being abandoned when Lawton gets the U-boat underway, towing behind it *The Freedom* and her bounty. When the three are spotted aboard *The Freedom*, The Sea Witch fires a cannonball, rendering the Grey Wolf incapable of submerging.

FULL SPEED AHEAD

Indy knows that Lawton is not about to go down without a fight, and so isn't surprised when the one-legged captain brings the U-boat about and ram's the galleon, sentencing her treasure to the unfathomable deep. No sooner does New Jersey Jones fish Cairo from the waves than Lawton lays claim to her. But Indy rushes in, armed with a cutlass against Lawton's Viking axe. Both men know that this time their vicious fight will end in death for one of them. They are correct: after Lawton hurls the axe into the sea, The Sea Witch riddles his body with rounds from the sub's deck gun.

Gasping for breath, Indy struggles to evade the crushing tentacles of the flesh-eating kraken.

Drifting into American coastal waters, the Grey Wolf is captured by the US Navy. Cagey Cairo goes back on the run; New Jersey Jones and The Sea Witch strike up a beautiful friendship; and Indy is left to tell Marcus Brody—yet again—of the riches that have slipped through his fingers.

THE WAR YEARS

WORLD WAR II finds Indiana Jones on the hunt for legendary artifacts in Greece and Ireland, while Hitler's war machine continues to grind away across Europe. The Golden Fleece, which once belonged to the winged ram Chrysomallos, had been sought by many, including Jason and his team of Argonauts. They believed that the power of the Fleece could place Jason on the throne. Equally powerful, the Spear of Longinus, or Destiny, was believed to have pierced Christ's side at the Crucifixion, and was thought to be capable of conferring great power on anyone who possessed it. As ever, Indy is not alone in these quests. Nazis and madmen are never far behind.

THE GOLDEN FLEECE

In 1941, Indy unearths an ancient dagger in Greece. Rescued from pursuing Nazis by pregnant pilot Omphale Kiapos, the dagger is stolen by members of the Cult of Hecate. Indy and Omphale then visit Indy's friend, scholar Daan Van Rooijen. Van Rooijen believes the Hecate cultists are on the trail of the Golden Fleece. They need the dagger to enact a ritual that will resurrect the Fleece's energy, and empower what remains of the Ottoman Empire.

A LIFE'S WORK

Van Rooijen has spent his life searching for the Golden Fleece, which has fallen into the hands of a would-be artist named Mehmed Sarper, who used the Fleece as the back for one of his canvases. With the Fleece in hand, Indy and Omphale are betrayed by Van Rooijen, who doesn't want it to sit in a museum. Neither, however, do the Hecate cultists, who kill the Dutchman and flee for Colchis to enact the resurrection ritual.

Indy has no time to discuss archaeology with the cultists and takes matters into his own hands.

IN THE FOOTSTEPS OF JASON

Days of tough travel bring Indy and Omphale to the Valley of Hecate, where a spring blizzard seems intent on foiling their efforts. They come upon the cultists in the midst of plunging the ancient dagger into the Fleece. But before Indy can act, Omphale goes into labor. At the same time, the Fleece's protector—a towering serpent—rises from the snow-covered ground, only to vanish, along with the Fleece, when Indy proffers Omphale's newborn son to the spirit of Hecate.

O GREAT MOTHER! HONOR THIS PURITY... THIS INNOCENCE...THIS *CHILD!* TAKE *BACK* WHAT IS *YOURS!*

Indy has seen stranger things in his time, but not many, and not for a long while.

SPEAR OF DESTINY

With World War II winding down and the Nazis on the run, Indy is excavating an ancient site near New Grange, Ireland. Following the arrival of a mysterious young Irish woman bearing a letter from Indy's father, Indy experiences a vision in which a spirit asks Indy to find the spear that bleeds, lest it fall into the hands of those who would drown the world in blood. Coincidentally, the letter from Henry Sr., who is in England, explains that a group of Nazis have expressed interest in locating the Spear of Longinus, which pierced the side of Christ at the crucifixion. No sooner has Indy read the letter than he is pursued by Irish "blueshirt" Fascists who are being headed by a Nazi leader.

GOINGS-ON IN GLASTONBURY

Indy and an Irishman named Brendan O'Neal seek out Henry and learn more about the mythical spear. The Nazis already have the spear point, but lack the wooden shaft. Indy tries to sway the son of the Nazi leader over to his side, only to learn that young Siegfried has been groomed to accomplish what Hitler has failed to achieve. Captured, Indy, Henry, and Brendan escape with the help of an English botany teacher, who gives them a cutting from a thorn tree that grew from the staff of the Spear.

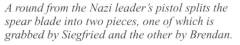

A round from the Nazi leader's pistol splits the spear blade into two pieces, one of which is grabbed by Siegfried and the other by Brendan.

Even half a blade proves better than none for Indy when a Nazi bullet making a beeline for him strangely changes course. Indy and the others try to outrun their adversaries, but a flat tire sabotages their escape, and Henry and the driver, Rebecca, are taken hostage.

NEVER A DULL MOMENT

In Wales, Indy has another vision, in which he is urged to continue the search for the spear and warned of imminent danger. The latter comes at the hands of the Nazis, who capture Henry and Rebecca, and try to drown Indy in a lake. Luckily, the lake bottom is a treasure trove of Celtic weapons, one of which Indy uses to sever his bindings. Meanwhile, the two halves of the splintered spear keep passing between Indy's group and the Nazis. At a ferry crossing to Ireland, Indy and Brendan free Henry, but Rebecca remains a prisoner.

CALENDAR STONE

In Ireland, back where he started from, Indy rescues Rebecca by getting the blueshirts to turn on their Nazi confederates. The pair then rendezvous with Henry and Brendan at the New Grange archaeological site, where, with a spear fashioned from one half of the fractured blade, a sprig of the original thorn tree, and a shaft carved from yew wood, Brendan activates the ancient powers of a spiral-adorned calendar stone. When the Nazis show up, the second half of the spear point flies to join its mate, and the tip drips blood. So, too, do all but one of the Nazis, who bleed to death as an earthquake buries the calendar stone—and those who would have used its powers to dominate the world.

The spear tip had been stolen and was found in a Nazi bunker. Indy wonders if the spear was partly responsible for the atomic bomb dropped on Japan.

POST-WAR WORLD

WORLD WAR TWO HAS ENDED and Indy is in the Soviet sector of multi-partitioned Berlin searching through the bombed ruins of a monastery for artifacts that may have once belonged to alchemist Albertus Magnus. With staircases crumbling beneath his boots, and spikes springing from the stone walls, Indy discovers an ancient cylindrical scroll and a medieval alchemist's bench that appears to have once held a trio of objects. Though he is in Berlin at the behest of the Soviet Artifacts Evaluation Commission, Indy is arrested by Comrade Major Nadia Kirov, who confiscates all his finds.

Accused of being a Nazi thief, Indy is put in jail with Dunkelvolk, a competitor for the scroll. Dunkelvolk is in league with Jäger, a Nazi scientist known for conducting reanimation experiments.

IN SEARCH OF THE PAST

Marcus Brody determines that the scroll, penned in reverse script, contains information about the Philosophers' Stone. This stone has the power to turn base metal into gold, as well as bring inanimate objects to life. Written in the 13th century by Magnus, the scroll reveals that the stone had split into three pieces that once sat on the alchemist's bench. These three artifacts are hidden in monasteries in Kiev, Ireland, and Tibet. Indy travels to Russia, discovering the first piece in a vast ice cavern beneath the monastery, gripped in the golden hands of an abbot who was turned to gold.

Indy goes to Ireland and collects an ancient cup from a coven of druids. They are not to keen to see it go and Indy doses one of them with a fluid that literally binds her to the earth.

TIBETAN TREASURES

In Tibet, Indy treks high into the Himalayas with a Sherpa guide named Zhaba to reach the Monastery of the Butterflies. There, a seemingly innocent cup of tea sends him on a psychedelic time-warp trip, during which he defeats a series of spirit opponents. Having proved himself worthy, he is granted the third alchemical piece by an aged lama, who tells him that the artifacts have the power to raise the dead or annihilate the living.

Resurrected Nazi soldiers comprise a zombie army that the Nazis plan to let loose on the world.

CRISIS OF CONSCIENCE

In possession of all three artifacts, Indy feels as if he's carrying a bomb. Averse to giving the pieces to any government, he returns to Berlin to seek Marcus's counsel. Nadia intervenes, however, seizing the artifacts as bait to lure Jäger into the open. But Dunkelvolk doesn't give her the chance. Ambushed, Nadia loses the items to Dunkelvolk, whose aim is to bring them to Koblenz, along with a shipment of guns. Fortunately, Indy destroys the armaments, though he fails to rescue Nadia from captivity.

MASTER PLAN

Indy follows Dunkelvolk and his fellow Nazis to a Gothic mansion, and ultimately to a medieval tower that rises above a vast cemetery where many German veterans have been interred. Under a full moon, the corpse-like Jäger assembles the three artifacts and succeeds in returning to life several dozen German soldiers. Acting quickly, and at just the right instant, Indy snatches the Philosophers' Stone from the alchemist's bench, and in so doing reverses its power, condemning the Nazi zombies to a second death and bringing down the tower itself.

Indy and Nadia flee the disintegrating tower while hundreds of resurrected corpses catch fire in the cemetery.

THE INFERNAL MACHINE

Sophia Hapgood re-enters Indy's life in 1947. Now an operative for the CIA, she enlists his aid in thwarting a Soviet Communist plot to unearth an ancient interdimensional device concealed in the ruins of the Tower of Babel. Infiltrating the Russian dig, Indy learns that parts of the device were hidden in Kazakhstan, the Philippines, Mexico, and the Sudan. He retrieves the pieces, only to find out that Sophia's boss is set on using the machine to eliminate communism and secure the world for the Western powers. Teaming with Sophia, Indy saves humankind once more by ensuring the interdimensional portal remains sealed.

Returned to life, the zombie Nazis stagger from the coffins, their decomposing eyes fixed on Indy.

A PROFESSOR'S LIFE

WHILE HE CONTINUES TO DIVIDE his time between teaching and searching the far reaches of the world for artifacts, Indiana Jones is beginning to feel that both the years and the mileage are catching up with him. Deeply affected by his experiences in World War II, he has become a more solitary, introspective man, at a point in his life where the losses greatly outweigh the gains. The world, too, has changed. Borderlines have been redrawn, former allies have become enemies, and roads and telephone lines have been pushed into what were once blank areas on the map. Most importantly, people no longer look to the past for answers, but to the future for salvation.

Happy to be himself, Indy still dresses as he did twenty years earlier.

HIS REPUTATION PRECEDES HIM

Following the recent deaths of his father and of Marcus Brody, Indy has found consolation in teaching and has published in academic journals. Celebrated both for his professional skills and his adventures, Indy is Marshall College's most popular figure: his Archaeology 101 fills up faster than any other course—female students outnumbering males by three to one. Trips to the Yucatan Peninsula and Guatemala have meant Indy has added three Mayan dialects to the languages in which he is fluent.

PAST PRESENT

Indy's classroom reflects his fondness for artifacts. Many of the maps have yet to be updated, and only brass instruments are permitted. In keeping with the times, however, Indy has developed an interest in cultural anthropology.

As if part of a museum display, Indy's adventure gear hibernates in his closet at home, waiting to be used.

Indy sometimes yearns for the old days, when Brody would burst through the door, and the game would be afoot.

DEAN OF STUDENTS

Indy has become close friends with Charles Stanforth, who replaced Marcus Brody as dean of students. While not the benefactor Marcus was, Stanforth is always on hand to intercede with Marshall College's governing board when Indy needs to disappear on an adventure. Like Indy's father, Stanforth often laments that Indy never married, and has grown weary of the US government's witch-hunt for communists.

GENERATION GAP

In Arnie's Dinner—surrounded by lettermen, poodle-skirted young women, and cliques of greasers, all bopping to a soundtrack of jukebox rock 'n' roll—Indy listens raptly to motorcyclist Mutt Williams as he spins a tale of intrigue and abduction. The tale involves his mother and his surrogate father, Harold Oxley, an old friend Indy lost touch with twenty years earlier. Mutt has come to ask Indy's help, on behalf of his mom, who claims to have met Indy during one of his adventures.

"It's been a brutal couple of years, Charlie."
—Indiana Jones

OBJECTS OF POWER

Indy's on-campus apartment is tastefully decorated with pieces of ancient sculpture, architectural details, shelf after shelf of rare texts, and countless souvenirs and artifacts, most of which have been deemed too insignificant for museum collections. Each object, however, has sentimental value for Indy, and serves to remind him of more action-filled times.

Bell jar contains the remains of a highly venomous snake.

Maori wooden figurine from eastern New Zealand.

Small sculpture of unknown provenance found in southern France.

New Guinea rattle fetish is made of bone, trade beads, and cowrie shells.

Miniature reproduction of a bust of Emperor Vespasian

Indy's first pair of binoculars belonged to Teddy Roosevelt.

Device for demonstrating Sun-Earth-Moon relationship

Graduated beaker Indy received as a gift from Marie Curie

Death mask obtained during a 1932 expedition to Iceland

Melanesian fetish is a gift from anthropologist Bronislaw Malinowski.

Shamanic carving acquired in Lagos, West Africa

Early-period orange-ware utility urn

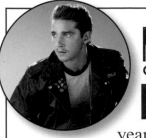

MUTT WILLIAMS

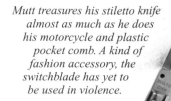

Mutt treasures his stiletto knife almost as much as he does his motorcycle and plastic pocket comb. A kind of fashion accessory, the switchblade has yet to be used in violence.

RAISED BY HIS MOTHER after his dad, Colin, an RAF pilot, died in World War II, nineteen-year old Mutt has spent the past few years trying on various identities—the latest of which is borrowed from actors Marlon Brando and James Dean, singer Elvis Presley, and any number of leather-clad urban rebels. A phone call placed in Peru by his mother prompts Mutt to climb aboard his bike and head for the New England college town where a certain Indiana Jones is professor of archaeology. Fortunately for Mutt, he arrives just as Indiana is about to embark on a last-minute trip.

ROCK 'N' ROLL SWASHBUCKLER

Mutt's carefully groomed pompadour, leather jacket, dungarees, and motorcycle boots belie years of attending a variety of costly prep and boarding schools. He spends much of his time fiddling with the intricate mechanics of his cycle. Whilst at school, he was forced to take classes in debate and medieval literature, and learn to play tennis, golf, chess, and fencing—all of which he considers useless skills. Nevertheless, he can handle a blade like nobody's business. Fencing champ for two consecutive years, Mutt was ultimately disqualified for gambling—on himself, to win. And while he chooses to pepper his speech with slang of the day, such as "ain't" and "man," he can quote from poems by T.S. Eliot and William Wordsworth.

WILD ONE

Mutt is too much of a loner to join a motorcycle club, but he wants nothing more than to become a motorcycle mechanic, and eventually a builder of customized motorcycles, which he sees as the future of transportation. He dreams of opening a shop in California, where he can devote himself to raising handlebars, lowering saddles, fashioning chrome exhaust systems, and bobbing fenders.

THE APPLE AND THE TREE

In Peru, Mutt and Marion Ravenwood are thrown together in an adventure that takes them into the Amazon rainforest, on the run from warriors with semi-automatic rifles and others with spears, blow-guns, and bolas. Marion shows herself to be adept at handling the most difficult of tasks, from driving a truck down a jungle road to piloting an amphibious vehicle through stretches of white water. What Marion can't handle, Mutt can, drawing on skills that turn out to be more useful than he would have thought.

STILL THE SAME

Indy and Marion Ravenwood haven't seen each other for twenty years. But when their paths cross in South America, it's as if no time has passed. Quickly they fall into the flirting repartee and mutual accusations that typified their former exchanges. It isn't long before Indy is wondering whether Marion has roped him into helping her out of the trouble she has gotten herself into.

"SHE DIDN'T SEEM SURPRISED TO SEE ME.

"AND SOMEHOW, *THAT* DIDN'T SURPRISE ME.

Mutt rides a modified cycle that will one day be termed a "bobber."

Mutt has traveled in Europe, but Peru opens his eyes to the wonders of the ancient American cultures, in which time-reckoning and stargazing took central place, and astronomical data was recorded in stone carvings.

OFF THE BEATEN PATH

At Chauchilla Cemetery, on the hunt for "Orellana's cradle," Mutt sees firsthand that Dr. Henry Jones is more the grave-robber he first understood him to be than the unassuming college professor he pretends to be. Throughout their time together Mutt is continually dumbfounded by Indy's abilities, and compelled to show that he is every bit as tough and resourceful—even in the face of scorpions, piranhas, and other biting things. Mutt learns quickly, though, that when Indy says "Trust me," that is usually the time to duck and cover.

> ## *"Mutt's the name I picked. You have a problem with it?"*
>
> —*Mutt Williams*

WHAT'S IN A NAME?

In addition to having to rescue his mother and his surrogate dad, Harold Oxley, Mutt has to face up to the fact that the world doesn't necessarily revolve around cycles, hair pomade, and shake, rattle, 'n' roll. Peru brings him in touch with a host of people who couldn't care less about all that, or about whether Mutt Williams lives or dies. The adventure also brings revelations that will shake Mutt's view of history—personal and otherwise.

Mutt wonders how this guy, Indiana Jones, had figured in his mom's life.

PERU ADVENTURES

BLANKETED BY IMPENETRABLE FOREST, furrowed by mountain ranges that rise steeply from the cold Pacific, and home to one of the driest deserts on earth, the South American nation of Peru has, through the years, become a steady stomping ground for Indy. The ancient ruins that dot Peru's three realms play an integral part in the adventure that brings him south yet again. From the mysterious Nazca Lines of the coast to the stone temples of the lush interior, Indy gathers clues to the location of a ceremonial center from which all the others may have evolved, and solves a mystery as old as time.

Enormous geoglyphs adorn the iron oxide-rich Nazca Plain. Designed for the gods, they are visible only from above.

BLOOD BROTHERS

George McHale, whom Indy has called Mac since they first met in 1939, is a former operative in England's secret intelligence service, MI6. Frequently partnered with Indy during World War II, when Indy served with the Office of Strategic Services, Mac has saved his friend's life on at least two occasions: once when the pair masqueraded as Nazis in an attempt to steal the cipher machine responsible for generating Germany's Enigma codes, and again in Jakarta, Indonesia, where Indy was shot with amnesia darts. Since the end of the war, however, cheery Mac has taken his fondness for women and gambling to the extreme, and can no longer be trusted to tell the full truth.

LINES IN THE SAND

Indy's search for Harold Oxley and Mutt's mother begins in Nazca, which lies in the shadow of the Andes Mountains, and is built on the ruins of an ancient culture. By day the small town teems with highlanders in ear-flapped caps and ponchos, bartering for goods in the market. By night the desperadoes appear, fueled on strong local liquors and homebrewed beer, wearing revolvers on their hips, and looking for trouble of any sort.

Just like Indy, Mac thinks as he watches his old friend. Never satisfied to leave well enough alone.

AS ABOVE, SO BELOW

At the edge of town sits an age-old sanatorium dedicated to Saint Anthony de Padua, the patron saint of lost things. Administered by a group of nuns, the building's barred cells house the mentally crippled and the criminally insane; as well as others who have lost their way—single-minded seekers such as Harold Oxley.

NO BONES ABOUT IT

The ancient Andean cultures revered the dead. Corpses mummify naturally in the arid conditions, preserving even textiles and the bodies of sacrificed baby llamas. Many of the ancient burial sites are still protected by the descendents of fierce warriors—places like Chauchilla Cemetary, situated on a promontory that overlooks the Nazca Lines, and rumored to be guarded by skeletal soldiers, whose blow-gun darts cause instant death.

Indy and Mutt's search leads to a 500-year-old crypt, which contains an astounding find.

"Stare into its eyes, and it'll drive you mad."
—Indiana Jones

THE "OX"

Born in Leeds in 1887, "freelance" archaeologist Harold Oxley studied with Indy at Oxford under Professor Abner Ravenwood, and later became a close friend of Marion. But Oxley didn't share Ravenwood's fascination for finding Tanis and the Ark of the Covenant. Obsessed with unearthing a crystal skull, Oxley focused his efforts on Central and South Americas, and for many years sought fearlessly to prove that legends regarding El Dorado were based on fact. A close friend of Indy's for many years, Oxley, without explanation, broke off all communication with him in 1937.

PROTECTORS OF THE FOREST

The Amazon rainforest conceals many secrets. Since Pizarro's conquest of Peru, rumors have persisted of the existence of a city of gold, known by the early conquistadors as El Dorado, and by the Inca as Akator. Built by the Ugha people with the help of their gods, Akator was said to have been millennia ahead of its time. The search for the city claimed the lives of many explorers and comes close to claiming Indy.

Ugha warriors are thought to have perfected the use of a throwing weapon called the bola.

Akator bequeathed monolithic architecture to the Tihuanacans; precision stonework to the Inca; corbel arch construction to the Maya; and ghoulish sculpture to the Aztec. An American Atlantis, it may be the source from which all other cities sprang.

A COLD WAR

IF INDY HAS LEARNED ANYTHING over the years, it's that the world will never be safe from groups of misguided people who would attempt to use sacred objects for malevolent purposes. Thuggees, Fascists, Nazis . . . and now the Soviets have entered the game. Traumatized by what Germany did to Russia in World War II and fearing the nuclear might of the United States afterward, Joseph Stalin had urged the KGB to experiment with the hidden potentials of the human mind. And now the chief architect of those experiments in ESP has emerged from behind the Iron Curtain to seek out an object capable of elevating the Soviet Union to the forefront in psychic warfare.

HANGAR 51

In their search for a suitable object, the Soviets zero in on a top secret government facility located in the high desert of the American Southwest, and they have coerced Indiana Jones into helping them root it out. Indy denies any acquaintance with the facility or the sacred object, but the Soviets don't buy it. Soon enough Indy finds himself in the familiar position of having to assist the bad guys in order to save the life of a friend. The enormous warehouse will prove to contain more than a few surprises, but in terms of the eminent Dr. Jones, the Russians will end up getting way more than they bargained for.

DEADLY MENACE

The commander of the Soviet Special Forces team tasked with securing the object is Colonel Antonin Dovchenko. Trained to carry out clandestine operations in diverse environments—from Dovchenko's native Siberian tundra to tropical rainforest—the soldiers are armed with prototype Kalashnikov combat rifles and Makarova semi-automatic pistols. A man of few words, Dovchenko takes an instant dislike to Indy, and is often tempted to supersede his orders that he should keep the American professor alive. Dovchenko has an equal distaste for insects, ants especially.

RUSSIAN DUCK

In addition to being well-armed, the Special Forces team has been outfitted with trucks, jeeps, and amphibious vehicles. The ZiL-485, known also as the BAW, is a Soviet version of the US DUKW, or "duck," an all-wheel-drive vehicle whose water-tight

hull is equipped with a propeller. The sturdy Soviet model features a front-mounted machinegun, and proves itself to be agile in rapids and whirlpools.

The centerpiece of the Soviet vehicular fleet is a wedding of tank and bulldozer known as a jungle cutter. In place of a gun turret, the treaded chimera has a shed-like operator's compartment and a V-shaped prow, reminiscent of a locomotive's snow-remover. This is fronted by a pair of spring-loaded and chain-driven cutting blades capable of chewing up and spitting out a meter-thick tree in a matter of seconds.

HEART AND MIND

Raised in a superstitious Ukranian village, where her psychic abilities led to her being branded a "witch," Irina Spalko was handpicked by Stalin to oversee research into psychic warfare. A former member of the KGB's Science and Technology Directorate, Spalko has been decorated with the Order of Lenin. Her powers of intuition have taken her a long way from the experiments she performed on animals as a teenager. As voracious a seeker of truth as any Indy has ever met, Spalko shows that there is no limit to how far she is prepared to go to achieve her goals. Her expertise with the saber, rapier, and foil drives the point home.

"We will be everywhere at once, Dr. Jones, as powerful as a hypnotic command."—Irina Spalko

BUNGLE IN THE JUNGLE

Indy has a gift for turning even the most carefully thought-out plan topsy-turvy. The more overwhelming the odds, the better. Before long, nothing is safe from the menace he's capable of causing: vehicles, specially trained troops, sadistic military officers, or highly skilled duelists. To Spalko, it almost seems that Indiana Jones has the ability to call on elemental forces to stand at his back and see him through episodes that would crush mere mortal men.

Spalko is not daunted. She has broken harder men, and she will break Indiana Jones.

BEYOND THE WORLD

In the films, Indy often goes it alone. In the real world, an army of personnel supports Harrison Ford and his fellow actors, for the *Indiana Jones* movies are collaborative efforts. Here, while Indy prepares to grab the golden Chachapoyan fertility idol, Ford's stunt double stands at the ready out of frame. Also on set are the camera crew (led by cinematographer Douglas Slocombe), the sound engineer, the script continuity supervisor, makeup artists, and a host of other technicians, gaffers, and grips. Of course, at the hub of all this activity, director Steven Spielberg waits for just the right moment to call "Action!"

THE INDY TEAM

George Lucas, Robert Watts, Harrison Ford, and Steven Spielberg in Marin County, California, while shooting pickup footage for the motorcycle chase in Last Crusade.

LIKE ANY WORKS OF ART, movies begin as ideas, which then need to be fleshed out, financed, developed, enacted, and realized on film. Celebrated filmmaker George Lucas conceived of the Indiana Jones character when he was first tinkering with ideas for *Star Wars*. Director Steven Spielberg found the concept so appealing that he abandoned his idea of doing a *James Bond* movie and agreed to make a trio of *Indy* films with Lucas. After Paramount Studios okayed the project, Lucas and Spielberg secured the talents of many of the exceptional people they had worked with on previous movies.

MASTERS OF THE UNIVERSE

Searching for ways to script a contemporary fairy tale, George Lucas thought back to the Republic Films action heroes who were a staple of Saturday matinees. His protagonist began to take shape as a mix of soldier, spy, scholar, and treasure seeker. Steven Spielberg came to the initial story discussions armed with dozens of set pieces he was eager to integrate into the developing plot. He was also excited by Paramount Studios' involvement. His first production company had been named Playmount, a literal translation of his German surname and also an homage to Paramount.

MADE FOR THE PART

Spielberg suggested Harrison Ford for the role of Indy from the start, but Lucas held back. He had already cast Ford in *American Graffiti* (1973) and *Star Wars:* Episode IV *A New Hope* (1977), and didn't want the actor to be seen as his alter ego. Tom Selleck was offered the part, but turned it down because of other commitments. Cast at the last minute, Ford brought to the role the same vitality and humor that defined his portrayal of Han Solo in *Star Wars*.

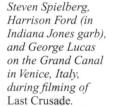

Steven Spielberg, Harrison Ford (in Indiana Jones garb), and George Lucas on the Grand Canal in Venice, Italy, during filming of Last Crusade.

RIDING HERD ON THE PRODUCTION

A team for more than 25 years—both on set and as husband and wife—Frank Marshall and Kathleen Kennedy have been the production force behind a host of successful films. They went to great lengths to supply Spielberg with all he needed to realize his visions for the *Indiana Jones* trilogy, whether it was elephants, thousands of snakes, or tens of thousands of bugs. They even found a mountain on the Hawaiian island of Kauai suitable for the dissolve shot into the Andean mount seen in the opening of *Raiders of the Lost Ark*.

Blockbusters credited to the husband-and-wife team include Poltergeist *(1982),* E.T. *(1982),* Jurassic Park *(1993), and* The Sixth Sense *(1999).*

THE INDY THEME

Celebrated composer John Williams has remarked that he wanted the introductory passage of the *Raiders of the Lost Ark* theme to feel "inevitable." Inevitable and memorable—as are Indy and Marion's love theme; Williams' use of atonal "fright" music; and the sonic transformations heard at the climax of *Raiders.* Weaving subtly through all three films, the original themes blend into inspiring orchestration and chorus work in *Temple of Doom*, and period drama for the Nazi rally scenes in *Last Crusade*.

Last Crusade *was Slocombe's final film.*

"The sets took a 200-strong team six months to build."

—Paramount

ASSISTANT DIRECTOR

David Tomblin, who died in 2005, is still regarded as one of the great first assistant directors. He began his career with Stanley Kubrick and went on to cocreate the TV series *The Prisoner* (1967–68). In addition to working on the *Indiana Jones* movies, Tomblin lent his talents to two of the *Star Wars* films.

WRITERS

During three days of discussion about *Raiders of the Lost Ark*, Lucas, Spielberg, and scriptwriter Lawrence Kasdan blocked out many of the scenes that eventually found their way into the sequels. According to Spielberg, Kasdan infused the first *Indiana Jones* film with a "Preston Sturges-meets-Michael Curtiz" sensibility. In their script for *Temple of Doom*, Willard Huyck and Gloria Katz, who had cowritten *American Graffiti*, drew on their knowledge of Indian culture. *Last Crusade* used the talents of Menno Meyjes, who had helped script *Empire of the Sun* (1987), and Jeffrey Boam, who wrote the screenplays for *Lethal Weapon 2* (1989) and *Lethal Weapon 3* (1992).

SOMEONE'S GOTTA DO IT

Apart from Harrison Ford, stuntman Pat Roach is the only person to have appeared in all three original *Indiana Jones* films. In *Raiders of the Lost Ark*, he played one of gestapo agent Toht's henchmen, then boxed Indy in the Flying Wing scene. In *Temple of Doom*, Roach wound up hanging from a ceiling fan and was later flattened by a rock crusher. And in *Last Crusade*, he was a zeppelin steward.

The fight scene in Raiders of the Lost Ark *was choreographed on the spot by Spielberg and Roach.*

Kasdan named Marion after his wife's granny, and found the name Ravenwood on an L.A. street sign.

David Koepp of Spider-Man *fame wrote the screenplay for* The Kingdom of the Crystal Skull.

DESIGNING THE INDY SAGA

Artist Edward Verreaux's Indy was based on classic western heroes such as the Lone Ranger.

SCREENWRITERS OFTEN PICTURE their films, even while the details of character, set, and action are vague and yet to be written. Executive producer George Lucas and director Steven Spielberg knew the look they were after for *Indiana Jones*, because it was inspired by the action serials and comic books they had enjoyed as youths, but they did not want to simply mimic those past images. They wanted to reimagine them for a new generation so they turned to artists and designers to interpret their ideas and to draw or model the characters and sets that they had in mind.

Veteran artist and film designer Ron Cobb sketched Indy as a truly larger-than-life hero.

IT'LL NEVER FLY

The task of building the Flying Wing for *Raiders of the Lost Ark* fell to production designer Norman Reynolds, who had worked with Lucas before at Elstree Studios, England. Basing his model on designs for a World War II aircraft that was never built, Reynolds costed out the Flying Wing at $1 million, but had a budget of only $750,000. Lucas inspected the model made by his effects company, Industrial Light & Magic (ILM), and simply snapped off two engines—quartering the cost of the craft!

IF ADVENTURE HAS A NAME...

When it comes to communicating the feel of the film to everyone involved, or even pitching it to a studio or distributor, advertising and publicity catchphrases can be as important as visual images. It takes a special talent to nail the essence of the story colorfully and in as few words as possible, and phrases like "Trust him" and "The Hero is Back" do just that. Used with preproduction art, the result can be as powerful a communication tool as a teaser poster to a potential audience. Lucas and Spielberg had final approval over all slogans used to promote the films, and Lucas himself came up with some of them.

The Flying Wing model

DRESSING THE CHARACTERS

Indy's costume of leather jacket, wide-brimmed hat, and rumpled trousers was inherited from the many action heroes who preceded him. To make the clothes believable and "lived-in," costume designer Deborah Nadoolman distressed Indy's jacket with a wire brush and a Swiss Army Knife, and had people sit on his Herbert Johnson fedora.

Artist Kelly Kimbal did many preproduction costume concept sketches for Raiders of the Lost Ark.

TRUE TO TYPE

Under the supervision of Lucas, Spielberg, and the studio, a design team struggled to create a logo that conveyed the bold, pulp look of 1930s' film posters without seeming outdated. First used on letterheads, the logo eventually appeared on a host of licensed items.

STORYBOARDS

Many of Verreaux's live-action and effects storyboards were based on stick-figure sketches provided by Spielberg. Storyboards would usually go through many versions before being finalized. It was then up to Industrial Light & Magic to create the final visual effects.

The Ark sits surrounded with mist, while Belloq and the Nazis hover in the background.

Indy and Marion are bound to separate light poles rather than back to back on one pole.

The fate of Belloq and the others is rendered in a more grisly manner than in the final cut.

Nazi soldiers disintegrate and evanesce in what appears to be blinding light.

PLANNING THE SET

Elliot Scott, who first worked with Lucas briefly during preproduction on *Star Wars* (1977), followed Norman Reynolds as production designer for *Temple of Doom* and *Last Crusade*. For the former, Scott designed the spike room and the mine car "roller coaster." His production paintings for the latter included an interior panorama of the Berlin aerodrome.

The aerodrome scene called for Indy and his father to wait in line for a ticket before they boarded the zeppelin.

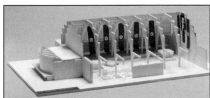

Scott's team built a preliminary model, or maquette, based on his painting of the scene.

Spielberg used the maquette to plan camera angles for the scene, which was filmed in London's Royal Horticultural Halls.

DRESSING THE SET

Spielberg and scriptwriters Willard Huyck and Gloria Katz delighted in inserting moments of "gross-out comedy" into *Temple of Doom*. Filmed at Elstree Studios, the Pankot Palace banquet scene contrasts elegant tableware and velveteen bolsters with rubber bugs filled with high-quality custard and rubber eyeballs floating in tureens of chicken broth.

Artist Jim Steranko made four production paintings for Raiders of the Lost Ark. *This one depicts a more rough-edged protagonist, with his bulked-up body and cigarette habit, but it brilliantly captures the spirit of what George Lucas had in mind for Indiana.*

SPECIAL EFFECTS

Paul Huston of Industrial Light & Magic (ILM) paints a forced perspective bridge for Last Crusade *by eyeing the miniature canyon through a camera lens (held in his hand).*

TO ACHIEVE THE NOSTALGIC PULP LOOK they sought, Lucas and Spielberg approached the *Indiana Jones* films as if they were products of the 1930s rather than the 1980s, and relied on the collaboration of teams of talented artists and craftspeople. Giving proper weight to the films' supernatural aspects sometimes required the use of technologies old and new in order to fashion backgrounds, add details, or supply phenomenal visual effects. Some of the effects used in *Temple of Doom* turned out so frighteningly well that a new category, PG–13, was added to the film rating system, in part at Spielberg's urging.

The climactic scene of Raiders of the Lost Ark *called for bluescreen technology, double exposures, and model-making.*

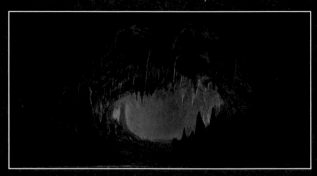

With computer graphics still in their infancy, exquisite matte paintings were created to conjure the volcanic eeriness of the caverns and mine tunnels featured in Temple of Doom.

NOT JUST SMOKE AND MIRRORS

Raiders of the Lost Ark's three principal villains—Gestapo agent Toht, Colonel Dietrich, and René Belloq—meet with gruesome ends, all under the supervision of ILM's special effects photographer, Richard Edlund. For Toht, a head sculpted from dental material was subjected to a heat lamp and photographed at one frame per second as it melted away. The sculpture of Dietrich's head was hollow, so that it could appear to be aging and caving in as air was sucked from it. Belloq's head explodes, but in order to ensure a PG rating for the film, some of the explosion was masked by the addition of a double-exposed column of fire.

MODELS AND MINIATURES

As *Star Wars* (1977) had shown, amazing results could be achieved by using models and miniatures, and the *Indiana Jones* films carried on the tradition. For *Raiders of the Lost Ark*, ILM constructed a miniature set of the locale where the Ark is opened. The thrilling mine car chase in *Temple of Doom* combined live action, shot on a full-size loop of track, with stop-motion animation and miniature mine car footage, obtained by running movie film through a 35mm camera. In *Last Crusade*, a model stood in for the World War I tank as it plunged from a precipice.

Visual effects supervisor Michael McAlister had a model of a plane fuselage career through a miniature tunnel in Last Crusade.

PHOBIAS ON PARADE

Unlike many members of the cast and crew, Harrison Ford was not squeamish about handling giant centipedes, tarantulas, rats, or snakes. But when cobras were added to the thousands of harmless snakes slithering through the Well of Souls in *Raiders*, a glass partition protected Ford from his venomous co-star. Right from the start, Spielberg was committed to using real animals where possible. While some of the rats in the *Last Crusade*'s catacombs were mechanical, that was only to keep the real ones from being burned alive in the petroleum-fueled fire that swept through the underground passageways.

SUSPENSION OF DISBELIEF

Built by British engineers who were working on a nearby dam, the suspension bridge in *Temple of Doom* was actually supported by steel cables. When electronically controlled detonators snapped the cables, battery-powered mannequins designed by mechanical effects supervisor George Gibbs flailed their way to the river, 165 feet (50 meters) below. Alligators stood in for the ravenous crocs. Gibbs was also the creator of the full-size tank in *Last Crusade*.

> *"Snakes don't bother me much. It's just acting."*
> —Harrison Ford

SHOULDERING SOME OF THE RISK

Although Harrison Ford did many of his own stunts and the colossal boulder was made of fiberglass, there was always a chance something could go awry. So, stuntmen Glenn Randall, Martin Grace, Vic Armstrong, and others doubled Ford in some *Raiders* scenes. When Ford had a back injury during the filming of *Temple of Doom*, Armstrong stood in for him for several weeks, and in *Last Crusade*, Armstrong jumped from a horse onto a moving tank. The famous truck-dragging stunt was performed by Terry Leonard. Armstrong's wife, Wendy Leech, doubled the female leads in all three films.

THE ILLUSIONISTS

Visual effects supervisors Dennis Muren (Temple of Doom), Richard Edlund (Raiders), and Pablo Helman (Kingdom of the Crystal Skull) had all worked with Lucas and Spielberg before. Muren, with nine Oscars to his name, pioneered the use of computer graphics to bring the dinosaurs of Jurassic Park (1993) to life, and worked on the original Star Wars films. Edlund, one of the architects of digital filmmaking, worked on Poltergeist (1982) as well as the original Star Wars trilogy. Helman worked on War of the Worlds (2005), among others.

Richard Edlund   Dennis Muren   Pablo Helman

SOUND EFFECTS

Having given aural realism to lightsabers and astromech droids in *Star Wars*, sound designer Ben Burtt found new challenges on the *Indiana Jones* films. Working with sound engineers Gary Summers, Richard Hymns, and Richard Anderson, Burtt made use of dolphin cries and animal screams for the translucent spirits in *Raiders of the Lost Ark*, .30–30 Winchester shots for the reports of Indy's handguns; and the noise of a station wagon coasting over rocks to enliven a rolling boulder. He made numerous recordings of Indy's whip, and squished his fingers into a cheese casserole to simulate ripping sounds. When rats in *Last Crusade* didn't sound squeaky enough, Burtt substituted chickens clucking, played back at high register.

Fond of "found sounds," Burtt rarely ventures anywhere without a recording device.

THE SAGA CONTINUES

Noted illustrator and art director Nathan Schroeder was responsible for some of the earliest concept art, such as his rendering of an African Queen–*style boat lazing by a river.*

IN THE NINETEEN YEARS since the release of *The Last Crusade*, several scripts for a fourth *Indiana Jones* movie were commissioned by George Lucas and Steven Spielberg. But the delay in finalizing production plans owed as much to finding free time in the schedules of Spielberg, Lucas, and Harrison Ford, as it did to their agreeing on a story that was faithful to the spirit of the original films and incorporated the signature elements: old-fashioned derring-do, visual humor, clever dialogue, romance, and dashes of the supernatural.

A TASTE OF THE NEW

Computer graphics modelled by Kevin Loo were used to illustrate a scene that features a rocket sled and bunker. Here, a sled with an outsized engine sits at the end of a run of Vignoles rails. Digital technology allows an image to be rendered three-dimensionally and easily manipulated to reflect color and size options. While this CG image was a good start, the sled in the film is quite different.

HOLDING FAST TO TRADITION

Notwithstanding leaps in computer graphics, motion-and performance-capture photography, animation, and other film technologies—many of which Lucas and Spielberg utilized during the intervening years in films like *Star Wars:* Episode III *Revenge of the Sith* and *War of the Worlds*—*The Kingdom of the Crystal Skull* had to stay true to the classic methods used for the earlier films. That meant filming at actual locations whenever possible, using talented stunt persons, and collaborating with teams of designers, technicians, and crafts people to build monumental sets. New names have entered the roster of production personnel, but the process of using concept art, models, and miniatures has continued.

This pencil illustration by Collin Grant shows a scene in David Koepp's script, which called for a convoy of Russian military vehicles to be shown from above, navigating a narrow jungle road.

TECHNO-CHIMERA

Concept artist Ed Natividad, who had majored in transportation design and illustration, was the perfect choice to conjure an image of a hybrid vehicle created from a tank and a tractor, which is capable of chewing up and spitting out jungle foliage. Natividad worked previously as a storyboard and conceptual artist on *Star Wars:* Episode I *The Phantom Menace*, designing architectural elements, costumes, and weaponry.

The jungle cutter's tall exhaust stack suggests that it has the ability to ford deep rivers.

EL DORADO

Koepp's script also called for an ancient city that drew on the architecture of several native-American cultures. In one of his first meetings with Spielberg, production designer Guy Hendrix Dyas, who lent his talents to *Superman Returns* and *Elizabeth: The Golden Age*, unveiled a pencil drawing that combines elements of Mayan, Olmec, and Teotihuacan building styles.

A miniature for the Chauchilla Cemetery, based on concept drawings by Dyas, was built by model makers Jason Mahakian, Tony Bohorquez, and Jeff Frost.

NEW FACES, OLD FACES

As many familiar names as new ones appear in the credits for *The Kingdom of the Crystal Skull*. Some familiar locations show up, as well, including Hawaii standing in for the Peruvian Amazon, and New Haven, Connecticut as the site of Marshall College.

Spielberg with Harrison Ford and Shia LaBeouf in Hawaii. It was widely reported that Ford, eighteen years later, still fit not only into Indy's shoes but his trousers. A newcomer to the series, LaBeouf shined in Holes; I, Robot; *and* Transformers.

Spielberg sports a Yale cap in New Haven, where he uses his iPhone to show animatics to his new production assistant, Justin Grizzoffi, and to his long-time producers Frank Marshall and Kathleen Kennedy.

Director of Photography Janusz Kaminski is a two-time Oscar winner for two Spielberg films: Schindler's List *and* Saving Private Ryan. *Kaminski was the cinematographer for many other Spielberg movies.*

Production designer Guy Hendrix Dyas on location in Hawaii.

MOVIE POSTERS

A SKILLFULLY EXECUTED POSTER supported by a clever tagline can be a more effective promotional device than an ear-splitting, explosion-filled movie trailer. Because posters aren't required to mirror reality, they are better equipped to capture the essence of a film by manipulating graphic images, compressing time, and encouraging the viewer to decode meaning. From the action-oriented poster for *Raiders of the Lost Ark* to the intriguing teaser for *Last Crusade*—which said that the man with the hat was back, and that this time he was bringing his dad—the artwork for the *Indiana Jones* films have become instant classics, showcasing the talents of celebrated painters and illustrators.

THE LEGEND GROWS

The poster for *Temple of Doom* says it all. The image of Indy with his shirt open, fedora in place, a saber resting almost casually on his shoulder is underscored by the poster's tagline: "If adventure has a name, it must be Indiana Jones." The poster suggests that we're in for a rough-and-tumble movie experience, dark around the edges but romantic at heart. To achieve the effect, celebrated artist Drew Struzan used a black-and-white publicity still of Harrison Ford, which he color-tinted to give the poster an aged look. As a bonus, a spot-varnishing pattern can be found in the black border.

A NEW TWIST

Evocative of the archaeological framing used by Richard Amsel in the first *Raiders of the Lost Ark* poster, Struzan's artwork for *Last Crusade* centers Indy and his father in an action milieu. It anchors the four corners with secondary characters, including recognizable faces and some familiar-looking villains. The tagline suggests that, following the darker *Temple of Doom*, we're back to having fun, by "keeping up with the Joneses." Though this was the standard release poster in the US, it still bore the May 24th release date for the film at the bottom, something usually reserved for advance posters. A similar promotional tie-in poster for Pepsi was made for this movie. In it, Indy dominates the poster in a strong action pose.

FOREIGN POSTERS

In the same way that feature films are sometimes re-titled for foreign distribution, marketing images also undergo adjustments. In the poster for the August 17, 1984 release of *Temple of Doom* in Finland, Indy is shown on his own, his sword raised against unseen adversaries: "The hero has returned." In contrast, the poster for the Polish release of *Raiders of the Lost Ark* does not feature Indy at all. Instead, noted poster artist Jakob Erol relies on macabre, disquieting images to reflect the occult nature of some of the film's scenes. Several posters were created to accompany the 1984 release of *Temple of Doom* in Japan, but all of them made use of the traditional photo-collage style popular at the time.

Temple of Doom—Japan
Japanese graphic artists chose to draw attention to Indy's blade and remove his trademark fedora.

Temple of Doom—Finland
The artwork of Indy with his whip unfurled was used in international campaigns, but not in the US.

Raiders of the Lost Ark—Poland
Erol's poster, blending Indy's whip with a blood-red snake, is one of the most sought-after by collectors.

CLASSIC ART

Created by the late Richard Amsel—known for his work on *The Sting, Chinatown*, and other 1970s' classics—the poster for *Raiders of the Lost Ark* has by now assumed iconic proportions. The artwork has been used countless times in various advertisement campaigns to tout both the film and the entire *Indiana Jones* franchise. In this reworking of the original poster for the film's 1982 re-release, the prolific Amsel boosted the action quotient. However, because the artwork appeared on posters after the film had made its initial world tour, the classic image of Indy is seldom seen on posters outside the US. The international poster for *Raiders of the Lost Ark* was created by Drew Struzan— based on a one-paragraph plot synopsis—and featured Indy and Marion, standing side-by-side in heroic poses, with minimal representation of the Nazi villains.

KINGDOM OF THE CRYSTAL SKULL

As Drew Struzan's incandescent, almost 3-D teaser poster for the fourth movie makes clear, a hero may age, but an icon is ageless. Center-stage, Indy looks intrigued, and his stance suggests vigilance rather than action. But it is a not quite human skull that dominates the composition. Other skulls and human limbs can be found among the bas-relief glyphs and designs— this poster was revealed to the public in December 2007.

In 1982, Kenner Toys released a second wave of action figures modeled on characters from Raiders of the Lost Ark.

MERCHANDISE

PRIOR TO THE RELEASE of *Raiders of the Lost Ark* in 1981, companies had to be persuaded of the value of issuing toy lines that tied in with mainstream movies. Howard Roffman, president of Lucas Licensing, recalls: "It was a hard concept to convey. People understood what an action movie was, but there had never really been an action movie that became a phenomenon like *Raiders*, and certainly never an action hero like Indy." Times have changed. Companies now vie for licenses to create toys for a lucrative market that includes not just children but avid adult collectors.

AN INDY FOR ALL OCCASIONS

Most children have experienced the thrill of being able to take a much-loved movie idol on adventures of their own creation, or to arrange a group of toys to "freeze" a scene from a favorite film. Perhaps no movie hero is better equipped to star in such scenarios as Indy, because he crosses genres as easily as he leaps chasms. As well as being an adventurous archaeologist, he is also a swashbuckler, cowboy, soldier, and daredevil—and the licensed toys are designed to support every aspect of his character.

COLLECTOR'S CARDS

In 1992, Pro Set released a collection of photo cards based on The Young Indiana Jones Chronicles. The full set consisted of 95 trading cards, 10 3-D cards (with a 3-D viewer), and eight Hidden Treasure cards.

In 1995, Galoob released its Micro Machines *sets of* Indiana Jones *vehicles. They included the pontoon biplane, Pan Am Clipper, and German staff car from* Raiders of the Lost Ark, *the mine car, Ford Trimotor plane, and Duesenberg convertible from* Temple of Doom, *and the zeppelin, tank, and wooden motorboat from* Last Crusade.

To tie in with the fourth Indiana Jones film, Hasbro released a Mighty Muggs version of Indy.

Saber to wield against Irina Spalko

SIDEKICK ACTION FIGURE

Hasbro launched its action figure of Mutt Williams, from *Kingdom of the Crystal Skull*, in 2008. Wearing his trademark motorcycle boots and standing 12 inches (30 centimeters) tall, Mutt carries his two favorite weapon accessories—a saber and a projectile knife that launches from his hand. Mutt's belt is equipped with a sheath for the sword, which fits nicely into his hand. Mutt can test his skills against such opponents as the Cairo Swordsman from *Raiders of the Lost Ark*.

Switchblade for fighting Amazonians

CUTTING EDGE

Made by United Cutlery in 1992, the *Young Indiana Jones Chronicles* Adventure Knife came with a personal note from Indy about how he used the knife as a boy. Indy's hat and whip decorated one side of the knife, and Morse code the other. It featured a carbon-steel master blade signed by Indy, scissors, a serrated blade, and a combination can opener-screwdriver.

ADVENTURE HEROES

In 2008, Hasbro released a new range of collectible figures, each standing 3¾ inch (9.5 centimeters) tall, and sold in two-packs. Characters from the original trio of films include Indy and Marion Ravenwood, Indy versus German Mechanic, Sallah with torch versus Mummy, Belloq with Ark versus Ghost, and Indy with Idol versus Tribal Warrior. The characters drawn from *Kingdom of the Crystal Skull* include Mutt Williams, Irina Spalko, Colonel Dovchenko, and an Ugha warrior.

Indy, with removable whip and shoulder bag, chases convoy on horseback

BUILDING-BLOCK SCENARIOS

Lucas Licensing president Howard Roffman noted a "synergy . . . between Lucasfilm and LEGO enthusiasts." Following the success of the *Star Wars* playsets, 2008 saw the launch of four *Indiana Jones* playsets: "Race for Stolen Treasure," "Temple Escape," "Indiana Jones and the Lost Tomb," and "Motorcycle Chase."

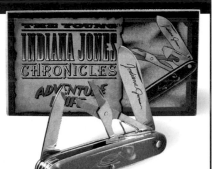

Convoy truck comes with an armed escort (a jeep with a machine gun)

Ark of the Covenant containing precious artifacts fits inside covered rear of truck

The 64-page Temple of Doom *special (1984) featured color stills and production art.*

PUBLISHING

THE WORLD OF *INDIANA JONES* has expanded into books for readers young and old, including fans of comic books, role-playing games, and armchair archaeology. Lucasfilm only allowed licensees to set their stories in a specific period of the *Indiana Jones* timeline. The novels, for example, fill the gap between *The Young Indiana Jones Chronicles* and *Temple of Doom*, while the Dark Horse comics are set after *Last Crusade*.

DARK HORSE COMICS

Brilliantly illustrated and faithful to the motifs that propel the films, the Dark Horse comics commenced in 1993 with a four-issue adaptation of the LucasArts video game, *The Fate of Atlantis* (1992). Hal Barwood, the game's designer, wrote the comic. The adaptation was followed by seven more miniseries, featuring cover art by Dave Dorman, Hugh Fleming, and others. Indy quests after the Golden Fleece, the Spear of Destiny, the Arms of Gold, and other fabled treasures in stories that usually span four issues. In 2008, Dark Horse launched a brand new miniseries and omnibus reprints of the highly acclaimed original sagas.

THE YOUNG INDIANA JONES CHRONICLES

Along with the miniseries editions, Dark Horse released twelve equally impressive issues adapted from *The Young Indiana Jones Chronicles* (1992–1993). Young Indy is depicted in adventures set in Austria, Mexico, China, Egypt, and Kenya; and then, during World War I, in France, Austria, and the Congo. Scripted by Dan Barry and illustrated by Gray Morrow and others, the adaptations are supplemented by biographies of historical figures and carefully researched accounts of the real events

GAME BOOKS

Bantam Books is credited with creating the game or adventure book with its *Choose Your Own Adventure* series, launched in 1979. The genre enables a reader to interact with the plot by exercising options at critical moments in the storyline. Ballantine adopted the format for its *Find Your Fate* series, which placed the reader in the role of Indy's younger cousin and which, by 1987, comprised 11 adventures. Authors included R. L. Stine, Megan Stine, Richard Wenk, and Ellen Weiss. Games publishers TSR, Inc. and West End Games also produced role-playing books starring Indy. In 1992, Bantam Books launched game book adaptations of eight *Young Indiana Jones Chronicles*, in which readers could imagine being in Indy's boots.

Nepal Nightmare Adventure Pack *was published by TSR, Inc in 1985.*

Find Your Fate #4 *was* Indiana Jones and the Eye of the Fates.

NOVELS

More than a dozen adult novels have been released over the years, including Ballantine's novelizations of the films. Rob MacGregor—reporter, travel guide, amateur archaeologist, and novelist of the occult—adapted *Last Crusade* and wrote six spin-off novels for Bantam Books. Pilot, aviation expert, and novelist Martin Caidin followed with two novels, and western novelist Max McCoy with another four. All twelve Bantam novels showcased Drew Struzan's extraordinary covers. Eight novels by German writer Wolfgang Hohlbein, with cover art by Oliviero Berni, are set after the film trilogy, but have yet to be translated into English. Adventure novelist James Rollins adapted *Kingdom of the Crystal Skull*.

Indy's investigation of a Scottish cave in Dance of the Giants *leads to a showdown with fanatical druids at Stonehenge.*

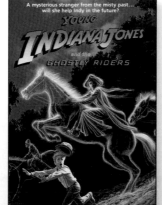

Published by Random House in 1991, Young Indiana Jones and the Ghostly Riders *is the seventh novel in a series for young adults. The adventure finds Indy searching for ancient treasure in Wales.*

FRENCH COMICS

In the early 1990s, French publisher Bagheera issued a trio of Indy comic books written and drawn by C. Moliterni and G. Alessandrini. (The first two were later reissued and given away at Shell gas stations.) Indiana Jones et le Secret de la Pyramide, Indiana Jones et la Cité de la Foudre, and Indiana Jones et le Grimoire Maudit are not available in English.

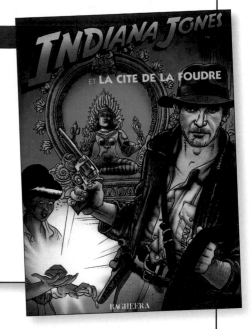

From 1991 to 1996, author John Malam used Indy as a guide to such ancient peoples as the Egyptians, Greeks, Romans, Vikings, and Incas.

MARVEL COMICS

Marvel entered the *Indiana Jones* universe in September 1981, with adaptations of *Raiders of the Lost Ark*. Then, from 1983 to 1986, Marvel published the thirty-four issues that make up *The Further Adventures of Indiana Jones*, along with adaptations of *Temple of Doom* and, in 1989, *Last Crusade*. *The Further Adventures* series features many of the characters from *Raiders of the Lost Ark*, including Marion, Sallah, and Captain Katanga, in entirely new stories. Artists included Terry Austin, Steve Ditko, Ron Frenz, and Ricardo Villamonte, and the scripts were by John Byrne, David Michelinie, Herb Trimpe, and Linda Grant, whose *Magic, Murder, and the Weather* is shown here.

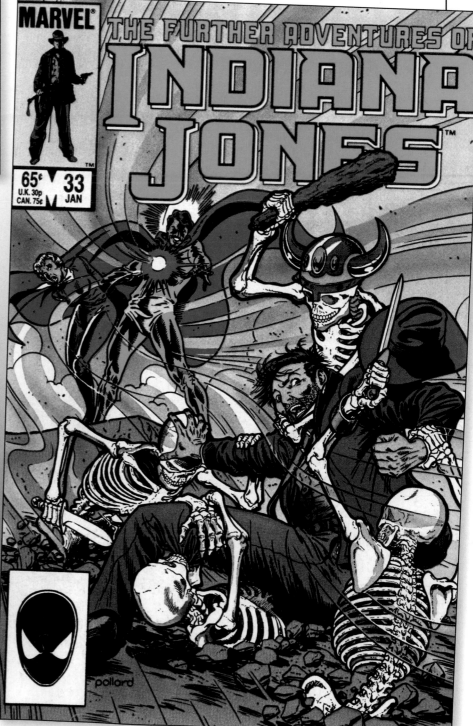

VIDEO GAMES

INDY'S FILM ADVENTURES were ready-made for spin-off video games. The action set pieces of the original movie trilogy served as the starting points for games that were played on a variety of platforms, from arcade games and consoles to handheld units and PCs. Some of the games were so plot-driven that they soon made the leap to comic-book adaptations, and many characters created for the games have since become essential to the official continuity. More importantly, video Indy—originally a mere ten pixels tall—has become increasingly realistic over the years, appearing in full-fighting trim for the 2008 game.

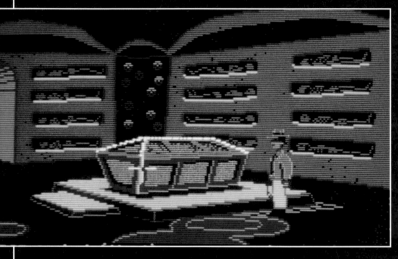

Neither René Belloq nor the Nazis appear in the Atari 2600 Raiders *game. Later games evolved into 2-D point-and-click quests that stuck closely to the plots. Released for various platforms,* Temple of Doom *features Thuggee guards and Mola Ram. By* Last Crusade, *players could travel with Indy to Venice, Iskenderun, and the Grail Temple—but games were hard to complete without help from FAQs.*

THE FILM TIE-INS

Until *Super Mario Bros.* (1985) shepherded the Nintendo Entertainment System into millions of households, home gamers had the Atari 2600, whose joystick was scarcely up to the challenges posed by the first official *Indiana Jones* game, adapted from *Raiders of the Lost Ark.* Two versions of *Temple of Doom* were created for Nintendo in the mid 1980s, with most of the action confined to the mine tunnels and Indy's search for the Sankara stones. Lucasfilm Games released *Last Crusade,* which featured bitmapped images of Harrison Ford and Sean Connery, on a floppy disk.

FATE OF ATLANTIS

LucasArts' *The Fate of Atlantis,* which built on the format developed for *Last Crusade,* is regarded as one of the finest graphic adventure games. It broke new ground in allowing players to choose from three separate paths (wits, fist, or team) in the quest for Atlantean artifacts, and in having dialogue options for Indy that affected the action. Originally released in 1991 on floppy disk, the game was reissued on CD-ROM two years later with a full dialogue track and iMuse sound. The game introduced a new heroine, Sophia Hapgood, who would find her way into subsequent games and comic books.

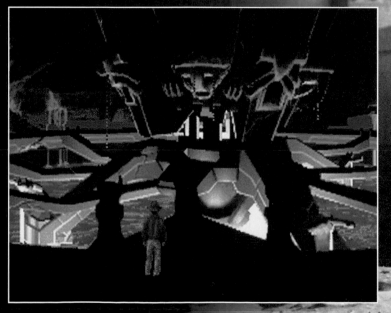

Thanks to SNES's Mode 7 graphics, Indy is constantly on the go, even fleeing a giant boulder that fills the screen.

GREATEST ADVENTURES

The advent of 16-bit consoles, such as Super Nintendo (SNES), allowed game designers to work wonders. Using the same engine that the *Star Wars* games were built on, LucasArts and Factor 5 released *Greatest Adventures* (1994), which had set-piece action scenes from all three *Indiana Jones* movies and vehicle-action play levels, accompanied by a stirring John Williams score.

DESKTOP ADVENTURES

Hal Barwood, the creative force behind *The Fate of Atlantis* and *The Infernal Machine*, introduced Indy to the Windows-using audience. *Desktop Adventures* (1996) enabled PC users to while away the hours completing one of fifteen quests, using the overhead perspective popularized by Nintendo's *The Legend of Zelda* (1986). Barwood developed the prototype on an Apple Mac, using programming language HyperTalk.

INFERNAL MACHINE

Rumors circulated among gamers that the sequel to *The Fate of Atlantis* would be *The Iron Phoenix* or *The Spear of Destiny*, both of which became comic miniseries. Instead, Indy wound up going head-to-head with *Tomb Raider*'s Lara Croft in *The Infernal Machine* (1999). The PC and N64 versions include beautifully rendered exotic locales, Russians as villains, and the return of the ever-popular Sophia Hapgood. The game combines a complex plot with realistic action, set to an evocative score.

UPCOMING GAME

Indy's search for his former college professor, Charles Kingston, in locations that include Panama and San Francisco's Chinatown, raises the bar on lifelike action in the upcoming game from LucasArts. It uses two real-time simulation technologies—Digital Molecular Matter (Pixelux Entertainment) and euphoria (NaturalMotion).

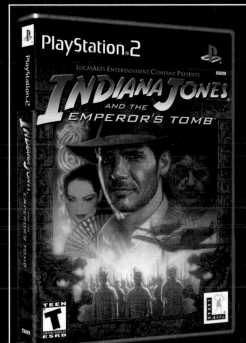

THE EMPEROR'S TOMB

Set in 1935, and thus a prequel to the *Temple of Doom* film, *The Emperor's Tomb* (LucasArts, 2003) sees Indy paired with Chinese operative Mei Ying. Together, they quest for a flawless black pearl buried in the tomb of China's first emperor. The game fits neatly into the official *Indiana Jones* chronology by providing background for Wu Han and Shanghai crime boss, Lao Che, the characters who appear in the opening scenes of *Temple of Doom*.

The play levels are set in fanciful versions of Ceylon, Prague, Istanbul, Hong Kong, and locations in China.

LEGO INDY

Targeted to appeal to the same gamers who enjoyed LEGO's Star Wars game—in other words, anyone with a sense of adventure and a sense of humor—LEGO Indiana Jones: The Videogame starred the familiar computer-generated LEGO building-block characters in recreations of key sequences from Raiders of the Lost Ark, Temple of Doom, and Last Crusade.

INDIANA JONES TIME LINE

GEORGE LUCAS ONCE REMARKED that his main reason for wanting to make *Raiders of the Lost Ark* was for the joy of seeing it. For Steven Spielberg, part of the pleasure of directing the *Indiana Jones* films derives from the fact that he is making them "for the audience." The conversation that resulted in their collaboration began with Spielberg's comment that he was interested in doing a *James Bond* film. At which point, Lucas told him: "I've something better." Yet with the casting of Sean Connery—the original James Bond—as Indy's father in *The Last Crusade*, the series of films came full circle.

1973 While working on the script for *The Star Wars*, George Lucas makes notes for the character of adventurer-archaeologist Indiana Smith, a tribute to the serials of the 1930s and 1940s that were stock movie-theater fare and which later played on television.

Late May/Early June, 1977 Friends George Lucas and Steven Spielberg discuss the project while making a sandcastle on a beach in Hawaii.

Late January, 1978 Lucas, Spielberg, and screenwriter Lawrence Kasdan concoct much of the plot for *Raiders of the Lost Ark*, based on a story by Lucas and screenwriter Philip Kaufman, in which the title character's name is changed to Indiana Jones.

Concept art by Jim Steranko.

August, 1979 Comic-book artist and illustrator Jim Steranko submits four preproduction "concept paintings" of Indiana Jones to establish the look of the hero.

June–October, 1980 Filming of *Raiders of the Lost Ark* begins at La Rochelle, France, using a submarine rented from the German TV show *Das Boot*. Sound and stage work begins at Elstree Studios, England. Location shooting continues for several weeks in Tunisia and one week in Hawaii.

June 12, 1981 *Raiders of the Lost Ark* is released in US theaters, to critical raves. On July 30 the film is released in the UK.

January, 1983 Debut of Marvel Comics' *The Further Adventures of Indiana Jones*, comprising almost three dozen issues.

April–August, 1983 Filming for *Indiana Jones and the Temple of Doom* begins in Sri Lanka.

May 23, 1984 Theatrical release of *Indiana Jones and the Temple of Doom*. The film is released in the UK on June 6.

UK poster. Art by Richard Amsel.

The creators of Jaws and Star Wars now bring you the Ultimate Hero in the Ultimate Adventure

1982 Though it fails to win an Oscar for Best Picture, *Raiders of the Lost Ark* receives Academy Awards for Best Sound, Best Film Editing, Best Visual Effects, and Best Art Direction-Set Decoration. The film also receives a Special Achievement Award for Sound Effects Editing. Later, a video game adaptation of *Raiders of the Lost Ark* is released for the Atari 2600 console and a VHS of the film is released.

1985 *Indiana Jones and the Temple of Doom* earns an Oscar for Best Visual Effects.

May, 1988 *Indiana Jones and The Last Crusade* begins filming in Spain, Venice, Jordan, and Elstree Studios.

1989 *Indiana Jones and The Last Crusade: The Graphic Adventure* and *Indiana Jones and The Last Crusade: The Action Game* are released by Lucasfilm Games. Nintendo releases *Indiana Jones and the Last Crusade* for the NES and Game Boy, and Sega releases it for the Game Gear.

May 24, 1989 Theatrical release of *Indiana Jones and The Last Crusade* in the US. The film premieres in the UK on June 30.

August 25, 1989 The Indiana Jones Epic Stunt Spectacular premiers at Disney-MGM Studios in Florida.

1990 *Indiana Jones and The Last Crusade* earns an Oscar for Best Sound Effects Editing. VHS and laserdisc releases of *Indiana Jones and The Last Crusade*.

THE LAST CRUSADE Executive producer George Lucas and director Steven Spielberg discussing shooting on the set of *The Last Crusade*.

CBM
AMIGA
A500, Plus, A600, A1500,
A1500 series (Minimum memory
required 1 Mega Byte)

U·S·GOLD

LucasArts' role-playing adventure game.

1991 Bantam Books publishes Rob MacGregor's *Indiana Jones and the Peril at Delphi*. This is followed later in the year by MacGregor's *Dance of the Giants* and *The Seven Veils*.

March, 1991 Dark Horse Comics' adaptation of LucasArts' graphical adventure game, *Indiana Jones and the Fate of Atlantis*, is published.

1992 LucasArts' *Indiana Jones and the Fate of Atlantis* is released. Rob MacGregor's *Genesis Deluge*, *Unicorn's Legacy*, and *The Interior World* are published.

March 4, 1992 *The Young Indiana Jones Chronicles* debuts on ABC, with a Movie-of-the-Week episode entitled *The Curse of the Jackal*.

Corey Carrier as Young Indy.

May 7, 1992: On *The Simpsons*, Bart reenacts the opening sequence of *Raiders of the Lost Ark* in Bart's *Friend Falls in Love*.

1993 LucasArts releases the CD-ROM version of *Indiana Jones and the Fate of Atlantis*.

July 30, 1993 Indiana Jones et le Temple du Péril—a roller coaster ride—opens at Disneyland Resort Paris.

Thrills and spills for visitors on The Temple of the Forbidden Eye ride.

October 11, 1994 JVC releases *Indiana Jones' Greatest Adventures* for Nintendo's SNES.

March 3, 1995 Opening of The Temple of the Forbidden Eye thrill ride at Disneyland, California.

April 1, 1995 Release of Dark Horse Comics' *Indiana Jones and the Spear of Destiny*.

1999 Release of the video game *Indiana Jones and the Infernal Machine* for Microsoft Windows (followed by releases for the Nintendo 64 in 2000 and the Game Boy Color in 2001). Voted number sixty-one of the top 100 films of the century, *Raiders of the Lost Ark* is selected for preservation in the National Film Registry.

October 26, 1999 *The Young Indiana Jones Chronicles* is released on VHS, in some cases with episodes combined and with the "bookends" featuring an old Indiana removed.

2001 The Smithsonian's Nation Museum of American History, Washington, D.C., adds Indy's hat and jacket to a Pop Culture exhibit.

April 21, 2003 LucasArts' *Indiana Jones and the Emperor's Tomb* is released.

October 21, 2003 A box-set of the film trilogy is released on DVD.

June, 2007 After over ten years of anticipation, shooting begins on *Indiana Jones and the Kingdom of the Crystal Skull*.

PUT YOUR HANDS TOGETHER Steven Spielberg and George Lucas make their mark on the forecourt of Grauman's Chinese Theatre in Hollywood, California.

October 23, 2007 Volume One of *The Young Indiana Jones Chronicles* is released on DVD, followed by Volume Two and Three in December, 2007 and Spring, 2008.

May 22, 2008 *Indiana Jones and the Kingdom of the Crystal Skull* premieres.

ON THE MOVE Shia LaBeouf revs up for his role as Mutt Williams in the 2008 release *Indiana Jones and the Kingdom of the Crystal Skull*.

INDEX

A

Adventures of Young Indiana Jones, The
  see Young Indiana Jones Chronicles,
  The
adventures of Indy's adolescence
  (1912–1916) 22–23
    as Boy Scout 10, 22
    decision to enlist for World War I 23
    finding of Cross of Coronado 22
    lion-taming 22
    on the circus train 22–23
    with Mexican revolutionaries 23
Alexandretta 98
Amazon jungle/rainforest 11, 117
Anubis 70, 71 *see also* Well of Souls
archaeological career, beginning of
  Indy's 16–29
archaeology as Indy's religion 67, 69
Ark of the Covenant 10, 11, 54, 62, 64,
  66–67, 68, 69, 70–71, 72, 74–77, 82
    and Belloq's ritual 76
    ceremony of 76–77
    contents of 76
    destructive power of 77
    en route to Cairo 73
    found by Sallah and Indy 70
    Indy chases after 74–75
    quest for 56–57
    re-interment of 77
    and Ten Commandments tablets 54,
      76
Aryan Culture, Institute of 87, 91, 93,
  94 *see also* book-burning rallies

B

Bamian, Colossus of 104
Bantu Wind freighter 75
Barnett College 104
  Indy as Professor of Archaeology at
    82
Barranca (Peruvian guide) 58, 61
Baudouin, Rèmy 23, 24–25, 34 *see*
  also World War I
Belloq, René 28, 59, 61, 65, 66–69,
  74, 76–77, 126, 136 *see also*
  Ravenwood, Marion
    approaches to Indy 67, 69
    attracted to Marion 69
    death of 77

finds Ark on mound 71
retakes Ark and Marion 75
unlocking Ark 69
Berlin 72, 81, 93, 94–95, 110–111 *see*
  also Philosophers' Stone
    and artifacts of Albertus Magnus
      110
    escape from 94–95
    and recovery of Grail diary 93, 94
Blumburtt, Captain 43, 44, 53
    book-burning rallies 86, 87, 93, 94
      see also Hitler, Adolf
    and 11th Puma Rifles 53
    and visit to Pankot Palace 53
Broadway and New York 29
Brody, Dr. Marcus 10, 62–63, 66, 85,
  88, 93, 97, 104, 107, 110, 111, 112,
  113
    as Nazi hostage 96
    in captivity 93, 95
    in Grail Temple 98
    rescue of 97
Brotherhood of the Cruciform Sword
  85, 86, 88, 89, 96, 100
Buddha, Covenant of 104–105
bullwhip 13, 45, 52, 58, 61, 71, 75, 104

C

Cairo 57, 106, 107
Canyon of the Crescent Moon 84, 96–
  97, 98, 100
    conflict en route to 96
    and Grail sanctuary 84
Capone, Al 29
Carter, Howard (archaeologist) 20, 21
Castle Brunwald 92–93
    as Nazi command center 93
    Indy's escape from 93
Chachapoyas 56, 58, 59, 60
Chiang Kai-Shek 105
Chicago, University of 64
    and Colosimo's Restaurant 29
    Indy at 28–29
    and murder of Big Jim 29
    and sax playing 29
children in captivity 40, 49
    digging in diamond mines 49
    escape of 52
Chimu Taya Arms of Cuzeo, golden
  finger sheath of 82, 83
clothing/equipment (Indy's) 12–13,

112, 124 *see also* bullwhip
  A-2 bomber jacket 12–13
  guns 12
  Herbert Johnson fedora 13, 124
  journal 13
Club Obi Wan 34, 36, 38, 45
collectors' cards 132
comics 134–135
  Indiana Jones and the Arms of Gold
    82–83
  Indiana Jones and the Golden
    Fleece, 108–109
  Indiana Jones and the Iron Phoenix,
    110–111
  Indiana Jones and the Sargasso
    Pirates 106–107
  Indiana Jones and the Spear of
    Destiny 108–109
  Indiana Jones: Thunder in the Orient
    104–105
crocodiles 52, 53
Cross of Coronado 10, 22–23, 80, 83, 106
Crusaders 98, 100
Czernin, Count 27

D

de Gaulle, Charles 24
del Arco, Felipe 82, 83
del Arco, Professor Francisca Uribe
  82–83
designing the Indy saga 124–125
d'Espere, Antoine 83
Dietrich, Colonel Herman 68, 69, 75,
  76–77, 126
Donovan, Walter 84–85, 87, 90, 93, 95,
  96, 98–99, 100 *see also* Grail diary
    and ancient manuscript 85
    death of 99
    in Grail sanctuary 98–99
    Nazi affiliations of 84
    and sandstone tablet 84, 98
    shoots Henry in Grail Temple 98
Dovchenko, Colonel Antonin 118
Dunkelvolk 110–111

E

early travels (1908–1911) 20–21
  British East Africa 21
  Egypt 20
  India 20
Egypt 20

Indy and Marion in 66–67
El Dorado 117, 129
escape from Pankot Palace 52–53
Eye of the Peacock diamond 25, 29, 34–35

F

family of Indiana Jones 18–19
First Crusade, knights of 84
Flying Wing 72, 73, 74, 124
Ford Trimotor 33
Forrestal, Dr. 58, 60
fortune and glory 82–83
further adventures 101–21

G

game books 134
Gobler 68, 75
Golden Fleece 108
    and ancient dagger 108
    and Hecate cultists/resurrection ritual 108
golden forearm sheaths of Pachacuti 82–83 see also Lake Titicaca (Peru)
Golden Idol, search for the 58–59
Grail see also Grail diary; Grail Temple and Holy Grail
    crusade 80–81
    cup 87, 99, 101
    Knight 85, 99, 101
Grail diary 86, 87, 88, 90–91, 98
    Hitler autographs 91
    map from 93, 98
    missing pages of 93
    recovery of 94
    search in Henry's office for 90
    surrender of 85
    window picture in 88, 91
Grail sanctuary 87, 98–99
    and Great Seal 87, 101
    Henry shot in the 98
    Indy in the 98, 100
    map of 100–101
Grail Temple 93, 98–99, 100–101, 136
    see also Grail cup and Holy Grail
    challenges and traps 90, 100
    cup remains in sanctuary 99
    and map to sanctuary 95
Great Wall of China 33
Great War, The (1916–1917) see World War I

Green, Harold 25
grenade launcher 76

H

Hapgood, Sophia 104–105, 136, 137
Hasbro toys 132–133
Hatay 81, 98
    and conflict in desert 96–97
Hatay, Sultan of 95
    troops and armaments of 96–97
Havelock 22
Hearst, William Randolph 23
Hemingway, Ernest 29
Herman 22
Himalayan Mountains 57, 65
Hitler, Adolf 68, 76, 84, 85, 86, 91, 94, 109
Hollywood 29
Holy Grail 78, 84–85, 86, 89, 100–101 see also Grail; Grail diary and Grail Temple
    healing powers of 85, 101
    quest as race against evil 93
    search for 93
Hovitos (Chachapoyan warriors) 58–59, 61

I

Inca 60, 72, 117
India 39, 40–41
    Pindari Glacier 32, 39
    Siwalik Range mountains 33, 38
    Yamuna River 32
Indiana (Indy's dog) 18
Indy Team: behind the scenes 122–123
Infernal Machine, The 111, 137
Iskenderun 63, 81, 93, 98, 136

J

Jäger 110–111
Jones, Anna 18–19
    death of 18
Jones family world tour 16
Jones Sr., Henry 18–19, 22, 62–63, 78, 84, 85, 88–93, 96–97, 103, 109
    abduction of 80, 90
    captive in Castle Brunwald 92
    and conflict with Indy 10, 92–93
    escapes with Indy from Berlin 94–95
    fear of rats 10
    and Grail diary 84, 85, 87, 88, 90–

91, 98 see also Grail diary
    and Indy's killing of Nazi soldiers 85
    Indy's search for 86
    inside tank 97
    obsession with Holy Grail 18
    rescued by Sallah 97
    revived by Holy Grail 85
    shot by Indy 85
    and studies of the Holy Grail 18
    talks with Indy on zeppelin 90, 94

K

Kali, Dr. Patar 104, 105
Kali Ma 36, 37, 41, 45, 47, 48–49
    blood of 50 see also magma
    dark sleep of 49, 51, 52
    Indy drinks blood of 49
    statue 42
    temple to 42
Kao Kai 34–35
Karl I, Emperor of Austria 27
Katanga, Simon 75
Kenner toys 132
Khamal 104–105
Kiapos, Omphale 108
Kingdom of the Crystal Skull, The 112–118, 128
Kingston, Charles 137
Kirov, Nadia 110–111 see also Philosophers' Stone
    captured by Dunkelvolk 111
    takes and loses Philosopher's Stone 111
Knights Templar 87
    and chalice from Constantinople 87
kryta (voodoo) dolls 49, 52
Kyojo, General Masashi 104, 105

L

Lal, Chatter 43, 44–45, 48, 49 see also Thuggee, the
Lao Che 34–38, 53, 137 see also Chen and Kao Kai
    and cremation ashes 34
Lao Che Air Freight 38
Lake Titicaca (Peru) 82–83
    and appearance of spirit advisor 83
    flooding of 83
    Indy led to island and lost city of 83
Last Crusade, The 78–101, 127, 136, 138
Lawrence of Arabia (T.E. "Ned" Lawrence) 21, 23, 27

INDEX

Lawton, Captain Bill 106–107
Lego 133, 137
Lindsey, Jock 59, 61
   and biplane 61
   and pet snake Reggie 59
Lotus Eaters nightclub 34
Lucas, George 122–123, 124–125,
   126, 128, 138–139

M

McHale, George 116
magma 48
   as antidote to Kali-Ma blood 49
   in abysses 52
   pit 51
Magnus, Albertus 110
Malinowski, Bronislaw 25
map from Grail diary 93, 95, 98
map of Grail Crusade 80–81
Map Room in Well of Souls 70 see
   also Well of Souls
Marhan 39, 40–41
Marshall College 57, 112–113
Mayapore village 40–41, 53 see also
   children in captivity
   shrine of Sankara Stones 48
merchandising: toys and games 132–133
MI6 93, 116
Micro Machines Indiana Jones toy
   vehicles 132
Mighty Muggs Indy toy 132
mines below Thuggee temple 49
Mola Ram 36, 48, 49, 50, 51, 52–53, 136
   death of 53
Moses' ram's head staff, replica of 76
movie posters 130–131
music (the Indy theme) 123

N

Nazis 54, 62, 65, 67, 69, 70, 74–76, 80,
   90, 92–93, 94, 95, 96–97, 109, 111,
   116, 136
   at Castle Brunwald 92–93
   and Grail diary 92
   and Irish Fascists 109
Nepal 54, 104
Ness, Eliot 28, 29
Nevada 11, 56
New Jersey Jones 106, 107

New York City 29, 80
novels 135
Nurhachi 34

O

O'Neal, Brendan 109
Oxley, Harold 113, 115, 116–117

P

Pachacuti, Emperor 82–83
   golden forearm sheaths of 82–83
Pan Am Clipper 56
Pankot Palace 30, 36, 40–47, 50–51
   arrival at 42–43
   assassin at 45
   banquet at 44–45, 125
   escape from 51, 52–53
   secrets of 45
   spike room 50
   surveillance at 44
   to the bridge 50–51
   and vampire bats 43
Peking, Indy's illness in 19
Peru 11, 82–83, 114–117
   and Chauchilla Cemetery 115, 117,
      129
   and George McHale 116
   Indy, Mutt, and Marion in 114–115
   and Nazca 116
   search for Oxley and Matt's mother
      in 116
Philosophers' Stone 110–111
   recovered by Indy 111
   reversal of power of 111
Picasso, Pablo 19, 26
post-war/peacetime (1946–1950) 110–
   111
Prentiss, Vicky 24
Princeton University 16, 18, 58
   Henry Jones' office in 90
   Indy's return to 28
publishing 134–135

R

Raiders of the Lost Ark 54–77, 124,
   125, 126, 130–131, 132, 138
Raven, The 64–65
Ravenwood, Abner 62, 64, 72, 77, 117
   rumors of survival of 65
Ravenwood, Marion 62, 64–65, 72, 74,
   75, 114, 117, 120

and Capuchin monkey 66, 67
falls into Well of Souls 71
and father's bronze medallion 64, 65,
   67
found in Belloq's tent 70
in Egypt 66–67
Indy's remorse over 67
kidnapping of 67, 69, 75
and René Belloq 65, 70, 75
and reunion with Indy 65, 66–67,
   76–77
Red Baron 25
Ring of Osiris 62
Russia and Cold War (and) 118–119
   Hangar 51 116
   jungle cutters 119, 128
   psychic warfare 116
   vehicles 118, 128

S

sabers 52–53
Sajnu 42
Sallah, Mohammed Faisel el-Kahir 63,
   66–67, 72, 74, 96, 99
   and adventures with Indy 66
   rescues Henry 97
Sallah's family 66, 67
Sankara Stones 41, 47, 48–49, 52–53
Sargasso Sea 106–07 see also Sea Witch
   Grey Wolf U-boat in 107
   Indy mired in 106
   and Lawton mutiny 106–07
   pirates 106–07
Satipo 58, 61
Schneider, Dr. Elsa 85, 86–87, 88, 100
   at Castle Brunwald 92–93
   death of 87
   and Donovan's tablet 86
   and Henry Jones Sr. 86, 87
   hunting for Brody 93
   in Grail Temple 99
   and Indy 86, 87
Schweitzer, Dr. Albert 25
Scott, Willie (Wilhelmina) 34–37,
   40–41, 42, 44–45, 46, 47, 49, 51
   and escape from Pankot 52
   and romance with Indy 45, 53
Sea Witch 106–107
Sepoy Mutiny (1857) 42, 47
Serpent Lady 105
set, dressing and planning the 125

Seymour, Helen 19
Shanghai 33, 36–37
    escape from 38–39
Shishaq, King 70
Shiva, golden statue of 82
Shiva god/life force 40–41
Shiva Linga sacred stone 40–41
Short Round (Wan Li) 11, 36–37,
    38–39, 42, 43, 44, 47, 51, 52–53
    and baby elephant 53
    and Duisenberg Auburn convertible
        37–38
    in captivity with children 49
    and magma antidote 49
    signature gear 49
    and Uncle Wong 37
Singh, Zalim 44–45, 49, 52
snakes 10, 22, 70, 71, 82, 127
    Indy's fear of 10, 22
Sophie, Princess 21
Spalko, Irina 119
sound effects 127
Spear of Longinus 109
special effects 126–27
    illusionists 127
    models and miniatures 126
    phobias 127
    sound effects 127
Spielberg, Steven 6, 120, 122–123,
    124–125, 128, 129, 138–139
Staff of Ra headpiece 69, 72
Stalin, Joseph 118, 119
Stanforth, Charles 113
storyboards 124
stunts 123
suspension bridge 52–53

T

Tahuantinsuyu (Incan city) 83
Tanis 57, 62, 64, 70, 72–73 see also
    Well of Souls
    archaeological dig 65
    Map Room 72
Temple of Doom 30–53, 125, 130, 137
Temple of Doom 50, 136
    from palace to mine 46–47
    spiked chamber 47
    Willie's bedroom 46
Temple of the Warriors 58, 60–61
    Indy and Satipo enter 61
    and parchment map 60

temple trek 32–33
Ten Commandments tablets 54, 76
Thuggee, the 40–41, 42, 43, 45, 47,
    48–49, 50, 51, 52–53, 136 see also
    Mola Ram
Tibet and Philosophers' Stone 110
time line (Indy's world) 14–15
time line (real world) 138–139
Toht, Arnold 59, 68, 69, 72, 75, 76, 126
    death of 77
Toht, Ilsa 59
Toynbee, Arnold 28
toys and games 132–133
Treaty of Versailles 80

U

U-boats 56, 75, 76, 107
Ur, tombs of 68
Userhet 70

V

van Aaken 104
Van Rooijen, Daan 108
    death of 108
Venice 63, 80, 88–89, 136
    escape from catacombs in 89
    Henry Jones abducted in 90
    Indy and Elsa in 88–89
    Sir Richard's tomb in 88, 89, 92, 98
Venice library 85, 86
    escape from fire in 86
    and picture in grail diary 91
video games 136–137
    Atari 136
    desktop adventures 137
    Emperor's Tomb, The 137
    Fate of Atlantis, The 136
    film tie-ins 136
    greatest adventures 137
    Infernal Machine, The 111, 137
    Lego 137
    Nintendo 136
    PlayStation 137
    upcoming game 137
Viking ship (on iceberg) 106
Villa, General Pancho 23, 105
visual effects 126–127
Vogel, Colonel 65, 85, 87, 93, 94, 95, 96
    death of 85
    and struggle with Indy 97
    and threat to kill Elsa Schneider 93

W

Wales 62
    and Indy's vision 109 see also Spear
    of Longinus
Well of Souls 70–71, 72
    escape from 71
    Indy and Sallah locate entrance to 70
    Indy in 70–71
    Map Room 70
    snakes in 70, 71
Williams, Mutt 6–7, 113, 114–115,
    139 see also Peru
Willie see Scott, Willie (Wilhelmina)
World War I 24–27, 34
    escape attempt with Charles de Gaulle
        24
    Indy adopts nom de guerre: Henri
        Défense 24
    Indy and Rèmy in French
        intelligence service 11, 26–27
    Indy and Rèmy on mission to Congo
        25
    Indy as courier at Verdun 25
    Indy as reconnaissance photographer
        25
    Indy captured: takes name Lieutenant
        Blanc 24
    Indy in disguise at Ballet Russes 26
    Indy joins Ned and Rèmy in 19, 23
    Indy sent to Palestine 27
    and Mata Hari 26, 27
    and Russian Revolution 26
    vintage tank of 96
World War II (1939–1945) 103, 108–
    109, 116
    effect on Indy 112
writers 123
Wu Han 34–35, 53, 137

XYZ

Xomec 59
Yama god 40
Yami, sister to Yama 40
Yamunu River 39, 40–41
Young Indiana Jones Chronicles, The
    16–29, 134
The Young Indiana Jones Chronicles
    Adventure Knife 133
zeppelin(s) 81, 90, 94

ACKNOWLEDGMENTS

AUTHOR ACKNOWLEDGMENTS
My sincere thanks to editor and author, Jonathan Rinzler, of LucasBooks, and president of Lucas Licensing, Howard Roffman, for thinking of me for this project; to Simon Beecroft, publishing manager of Dorling Kindersley Limited, for trusting me; and to my agent Eleanor Wood, of Spectrum Literary Agency, for representing me.

During the course of writing the guide I watched and re-watched the Indiana Jones films, The Young Indiana Jones Chronicles, and numerous documentaries. I read and consulted the film scripts, the novelizations, the dozen mass-market tie-in novels, the Marvel and Dark Horse Comics issues, many of the young-adult novels and adventure books, and West End Games' sourcebooks for Raiders of the Lost Ark and Temple of Doom.

I am indebted to the authors of all these works, especially to Jim Rollins, who let me have a look at his adaptation of Indiana Jones and the Kingdom of the Crystal Skull.

In addition I perused dozens of Indiana Jones websites, many of which are rich in detail. But I want to acknowledge three in particular: TheRaider.net, IndyGear.com, and Lon Mills' ihatesnakes.com. Lon was kind enough to help out with the text for the page on merchandise.

At LucasBooks and LucasArts, I also want to express my gratitude to game designer Tony Rowe, who provided me with excellent information about the Indiana Jones videogames; senior manager of Global Product Development, Chris Gollaher, who did the same for the spread on merchandise; Keeper of the Indycron, Leland Chee; Internet Content Manager, Pablo Hidalgo; director of publishing, Carol Roeder; and executive editor, Sue Rostoni. I want to thank Pete Vilmur, senior editor at Lucas Online, who helped immensely with the posters page.

Like the films, this book is a collaborative effort, and much of the credit goes to the people I worked with directly at Dorling Kindersley; chiefly, senior editor Laura Gilbert, who polished my often rambling sentences and always came up with terrific ideas; senior designer Jill Clark and designers Hanna Ländin and Ron Stobbart, especially for the time they devoted to the illustrations and the maps—the former executed to perfection, as ever, by Richard Chasemore and Richard Bonson; designers Dan Bunyan and Lynne Moulding; brand manager Lisa Lanzarini; and senior editor Lindsay Kent.

Finally, my thanks to Steven Spielberg and George Lucas for creating Indy, and the perpetually dazzling world he inhabits.

LUCASFILM ACKNOWLEDGMENTS
A special thanks to Steven Spielberg and George Lucas

Troy Alders, Matthew Azeveda, Guy Hendrix Dyas, Lynne Hale, Melissa Kates, Kevin Kurtz, Shia LaBeouf, Stacey Leong, Marvin Levy, Kristie Macosko, Tina Mills, Carol Roeder, Howard Roffman, Tony Rowe, and Pete Vilmur.

DORLING KINDERSLEY would like to thank Jonathan Rinzler, Leland Chee, Troy Alders, Tina Mills, Stacey Leong, and all at Lucasfilm; Richard Chasemore and Richard Bonson for their stunning illustrations; Innis and Christine Mason, and Lon Mills for merchandise photography; Clare Hibbert for additional editorial work; Marian Anderson for the index; Catherine Saunders for editorial assistance. DK would also like to thank the following creative talents for their contributions to this book: Ian Akin; Eduardo Barreto; Dan Barry; Gail Beckett; Bret Blevins; Danny Bulanadi; John Buscema; Chris Chalenor; Howard Chaykin; Sam De Larosa; Dave Dorman; Leo Durañona; Hugh Fleming; Brian Garvey; Jackson Guice; Paul Guinan; Lurene Haines; Matthew Hollingsworth; Ken Hooper; Klaus Janson; Karl Kesel; Elaine Lee; Frank Lopez; Mike Manley; Lee Marrs; Pat McGreal; Perry McNamee; Rachelle Menashe; William Messner-Loebs; David Michelinie; Al Milgrom; Bernie Mireault; Gray Morrow; Andy Mushynsky; Dave Rawson; Dan Reed; Mike Richardson; Alex Ross; Eric Shanower; Bob Sharen; Walt Simonson; Dan Spiegle; Ricardo Villamonte; Russell Walks; John A. Wilcox; Al Williamson; Stan Woch; Michele Wolfman; Gregory Wright; Andy Yanchus.

The publisher would like to thank the following for their kind permission to reproduce their photographs:

(Key: a-above; b-below/bottom; c-centre; l-left; r-right; t-top)

32 Art Directors & TRIP: Dinodia (tr). Lonely Planet Images: Sara-Jane Cleland (b). 33 Corbis: Bettmann (tc) (tr). 56 Alamy Images: Sandra Baker (tr). South American Pictures: Tony Morrison (br). 57 Alamy Images: Tim Graham (tr). Corbis: Reza Webistan (br). TopFoto.co.uk: Alinari Archives/Bruni Archive (tc); Roger-Viollet (bc). 80 Corbis: Yevgeny Khaldei (br); Underwood & Underwood/ George Rinhart (tr). 81 Corbis: Bettmann (br); Philip Gendreau (tl). Private Collection: (bc). TopFoto.co.uk: Alinari Archives (bl).